John Helmer was born in London and grew up in Essex. He has been (among other things) a top ten recording artist, a Perrier award winner, a cycle courier and a director of a telemarketing firm. He currently lives in Brighton with his wife and three children and helps run a press and marketing consultancy.

Forthcoming from Quartet Books Limited

Bowfingers

To Victoria

Mother Tongue
John Helmer

Best Wishes

Quartet Books

First published by Quartet Books Limited in 1999
A member of the Namara Group
27 Goodge Street
London W1P 2LD

This edition published by Quartet Books Limited in 2000

The right of John Helmer to be identified as the author of this
work has been asserted by him in accordance with the
Copyright, Designs and Patents Act 1988

A catalogue record for this book is available from the
British Library

ISBN 0 7043 8139 7

Phototypeset by FiSH books
Printed and bound in Great Britain by Cox & Wyman,
Reading, Berks

I acknowledge gratefully the support and encouragement given me in the writing of this book by the Helmer, Henderson and FitzGerald families. I also wish to thank Jennifer Johnston, and to record an affectionate tribute to the memory of my first ever publisher, Simon Dwyer.

The expulsion from Paradise is final, and life in this world irrevocable, but the eternal nature of the occurrence (or, temporally expressed, the eternal recapitulation of the occurrence) make it nevertheless possible that not only could we live continuously in Paradise, but that we are continually there in actual fact, no matter whether we know it here or not.

Franz Kafka

For Kate

Sweet

Salt

Sour

Tart

Aftertaste

Sweet

I

It was perhaps during one of Libby's epic telephone sessions that I overheard the story of how Lilith Hugg torched the master bedroom at Bearlands with a careless cigarette. Easy to do. Last languid puff before lights out, arm wilts on its way to onyx ashtray... Who would have thought that such an innocent piece of gossip could cause so much grief?

I see myself drifting through to the kitchen for a slice of bread, Libby's stocking tops snagging attention – my mother seemed to spend half her life on the telephone seat in that dark hallway, legs up against the wall, skirt bunched around her upper thighs. Stocking tops notwithstanding, the information would have lodged. Lilith had two sons at my school, one of them, Chrissie, in my class, the other the famous Boy Hugg. Information about Boy, information no matter how distantly related to Boy,

3

tended to lodge.

Two days later I was saying to him in the high street outside Boakes, *must have been a shock to wake up and find her bed alight*, and his eyes, pin-pupilled under vulpine brows, were tattooing a glyph of hatred on the backs of my retinas. Suddenly I was remembering, as he steamed towards us shouldering irate shoppers aside, that he wasn't the old mucker my tone had managed to imply; that I didn't in fact know him at all, except by reputation.

'Shut *up*,' hissed Libby, seizing my hand.

Boy flung her a reproachful glance. 'No, let's hear it.'

And I had no choice but to tell him what I'd heard or rather overheard about Lilith and her errant fag butt, and take the consequences. The consequences were appalling.

When I'd arrived at my state school the previous September – September 1975 – Boy Hugg had just replaced someone called Foxcroft as head prefect. The official version was that Foxcroft had fallen off his Kawasaki. 'Kawasaki my hole,' said Malcolm Finch. Malcolm took me behind Wentworth's spankingly whitewashed New Gym that break time and showed me a Turin Shroud in mural form.

'Boy did this?'

I watched my fellow fifth-former remove his specs to examine the sanguineous print of an AirWair sole. 'Split his nose, broke his collarbone in three places.'

'Why?'

Malcolm had one of those faces that look all wrong without glasses, like Action Man's hand without a gun. 'What do you mean, *why*?'

Boy Hugg was always hitting people: it was what he was famous for. He hit people if they got in his way. He hit them if they looked at him funny, or just if he felt like it. The question of whom Boy was going to hit next was always a live issue because difficult to predict. He needed no excuse, no justification. He was Boy Hugg, successful animal, alpha male.

Which was probably why, after a term of social obloquy, when I spotted him in the high street at Christmas outside Boakes the Chemist, I decided on a commando–style approach. Excuse me while I lift these hands from the keyboard and pummel my head.

At first I thought that the way his shoulders were vibrating had something to do with the cold. Snowflakes were falling around us, yellow in the sodium street lighting. Slowly, though, I became aware of him gazing at my mother with an awful intensity, slits of eyes scanning her pale, beautiful face as if seeking the precise bit of it he most badly wanted to hurt. 'Look, Boy,' I whimpered, cottoning on that something truly dreadful was about to occur, 'I thought everybody knew about—'

That was when he started screaming.

The tragic thing is that there was no real reason at all for us to be in the high street that afternoon. We had our dates, our nuts, our *Radio* and *TV Timeses*. The Christmas Eve dinner party menu had weathered a storm of reckless indecision and been finalized. But Libby had taken exception to my bumfluff – *I'm not having you put my guests off their food* – and Boakes in the high street was the only chemist she'd buy razors from. In the end we wound up doing the whole Saturday bit, including a by now obligatory footwear impulse purchase – a pair of foxy-looking black suede high heels.

'Aren't they *beautiful*!' she had cried, skirt parting over one thigh as she genuflected before the window of Ravel. 'They can't possibly be that!'

'You promised.'

'Hal, I only want to check.'

'Razors and home, you said.'

'Plee-*ease*.' Brows furrowed in imitation of my little sister Amy and a determined gaze locked with mine. From the next doorway along a gang of youths, all Brut and bleached denim, were ogling her with bovine, affectless absorption, but momentarily my throat-wanking, forearm-pumping peers – and in fact the entire precinct, with its boutiques and chaser lights, 'Bohemian Rhapsody' blaring out of every sound system, Kawasakis roaring through the underpass like stuck pigs – ceased to exist. I was conscious only of her dark eyes on my face holding an offer I couldn't quantify, let alone refuse.

Afterwards there were apologies. Apologies I accepted the way I accepted all my mother's apologies, with bad grace, scowling my way through our ritual coffee break in Planters.

'Are you *sure* there isn't anyone you want to invite for tomorrow, Hal? What about Anne?'

'She's got a boyfriend.'

'You don't have to stay in with us boring old farts – where do your friends go on Christmas Eve?'

'I haven't got any.'

She drained her cup, sighed. 'Well, I don't know what we're going to do about you . . .'

I took a look around the long low room with its liner-colonial décor, its dying clientele. Hardly crazy-teenager-out-on-the-edge stuff, but I felt a pulse of pure love, all the same. Did I want anything done about me? Libby stretched her arms above her head, swivelling male eyeballs. 'Come on then – Boakes.'

Of the few Victorian shopfronts remaining in this town of Miss Selfridges and Mr Byrites, Boakes was the most decayed. It stood in the lower, as yet unpedestrianized part of the high street, oblivious to the creeping of the 1970s down Pier Hill. Would that we'd gone to Boots instead. Because it was while I was hanging around outside afterwards waiting for Libby to emerge, watching the faces of shoppers come towards me, pinched with certain, uncomfortable knowledge – no more shopping days to Christmas – that I spotted him.

What followed was a movement as unmeditated, as careless of result, as those you see in nature documentaries: the turning of a flower towards the sun, the flight of lemmings. (I'd been unceremoniously dumped at Wentworth when we couldn't afford school fees any more, a despised neutral in a war zone of entrenched allegiances. Three months of friendlessness and isolation had sharpened desperation to a fine, impossible point.) 'Boy!' I called. Then again, more sonorously, so there could be absolutely no mistake, 'Boy Hugg!' After all, wasn't his brother in my year? Hadn't his father, a local printer, produced the letterhead for Housemartin & Son? Didn't my mother know his mother?

'Is Lilith out of the burns unit yet?' I called.

He turned in the methylated light of the chemist's window.

The Salvation Army band under the railway bridge farted

raggedly to a halt when the shouting started. '*Whore*' made them wince. At '*lying slag*' their chins dropped. They watched incredulously as the yob in the leather bomber grabbed the pretty young mother's jaw in a pincerlike grip and began to force the fingers of his other hand inside her mouth. They watched him struggle to trap her tongue; like a bar of soap or a live fish it proved elusive to the grasp. For one moment only he managed to yank the tip of the glistening muscle out between her jaws, as gagging noises began issuing from her throat, before she managed to shove him back and he was left pinching thin air. Her eyes rolled wildly from side to side as if seeking assistance, but despite their scandalized expressions, their muttered disgust, the musician/soldiers obviously weren't contemplating any physical intervention (it wasn't that kind of army). And who could blame them? Boy looked terrifying; spit flying, muscles in his neck veined and bulging. People were giving us a wide berth by now. People were stepping off the pavement into the path of blaring cars, in fact, to avoid us.

I felt my own neck muscles knot, my scalp pucker like a poppadum. Not so much because of the threat of injury to Libby – I never seriously thought that he was going to hurt her – it was that phrase, *lying slag*. It sent a ripple of unease across the hitherto unwrinkled pond of my reality, seeming to indicate as it did a past history; seeming to indicate, in fact, a whole Pentateuch of grievance and betrayal. I knew that my mother had visited Bearlands, because she was always ripping the piss out of its décor; but nothing had ever been mentioned about her meeting Boy there, or anywhere else. And I'd have known, surely, if she had a secret life, wouldn't I? Libby and I had always been as close as a mother and son can safely be. Closer.

Libby's reaction, or lack of reaction, did nothing to reassure me; in some ways it was the most horrifying aspect of the whole episode. Usually so condign when what she called her Paddy Blood was roused, handy with the tart, on-the-money comeback, she appeared suddenly lost for words. Boy ran on unchallenged until finally, like the toy without the Duracell, he ran out. There was no response. Not even when he stalked off, flinging her a last, almost plaintive '*Jesus wept!*' Her eyes didn't wander from the ground as the broad back ran the gauntlet of tutting navy, silver and maroon. Slumped against the window of Boakes, backlit by the cobalt neon Durex sign, she remained bafflingly inert.

I stepped forward and with a trembling finger brushed a violet tear of spit from her chin. 'What?' I said.

'What.' She raised her lids at me in cold contempt.

II

Mum was not usually the word.

We caught a bus home. We only ever caught a bus home when Libby wanted to punish herself, though the purchase of a pair of new shoes and some disposable razors was hardly splashing out. If something else had pricked her conscience she wasn't saying. The driver let us off at the traffic lights, slurring, 'Cheer up, darling, it might never happen.' She hardly seemed to notice.

From the lights, Cato Road careers downhill for a hundred yards or so before colliding with Somerville Drive. We lived on the site of the collision. Our house stood on a large corner plot thick with trees, screened from the street by hedge. The house had been built by an architect. In my father's eyes that made it good: Libby wanted to know what sort of an architect designs a house with six bedrooms and no dining room, so sparsely windowed and grim that you needed a torch to find your way around it even in daylight. Where was she supposed to feed her friends? And what was the stroke of decorative genius which could make the cavernous hall say anything other than *barn*?

Now, as she strode into the Stygian hallway you could tell by the depth of the thud with which her bag hit the telephone seat that the house was in some way to blame for what had happened in the high street today.

The baby-sitter stood up as we came into the sitting room, smoothing a dress of angora wool over crackling tights. 'Hello, Mrs Housemartin.'

'How's Amy?' my mother enquired.

'Not so hot.' Anne Singleton tucked a strand of hair behind one ear and smiled adoringly at Libby. My eyes wandered towards the nestled hollow on the sofa cushion, the pitched roof of a diet book.

'Has she eaten anything?'

Anne looked thoughtful at the mention of food. 'A bowl of Rice Crispies.'

'Poor thing. I'd better warm her up some soup. Thanks for coming in, by the way, Anne.'

'I hope you had a nice time.'

'Wonderful,' said Libby tightly. 'Listen, I'll get you your money.' She went out to the hall for her handbag.

Anne plucked the diet book from the sofa and clasped it to her chest, avoiding my gaze. There was a time when we'd played together (or rather, a time when Anne had locked me in her house and forced me to play with her). But now that she had these tits and went out with a six-former I had become invisible. Neither of us spoke during the minute or so Libby was out of the room. It was like time you spend

11

with strangers in a lift: time you pretend doesn't exist.

'Mind if I pay you tomorrow?' said Libby, returning. 'Only I'm a bit short of cash. I had to buy these shoes, you see.'

'They're beautiful, Mrs Housemartin...But they've got a bit wet.'

Libby's pleasure in her find had been childlike. 'My Christmas present to myself,' she'd lisped, counting out the pound notes; insisting that they *couldn't* be taken off again, *had* to be worn home. The assistant's warning against the slush must have rung in her ears; now as she turned her toe on the carpet, she grimaced at the salt-stained suede.

I began to drift towards the door. 'So how many ounces have you lost this week?' I heard my mother ask Anne as they followed me through to the hall.

'Ounces? Pounds!'

Pausing briefly before pushing through the green baize door into the kitchen, I watched Anne arch her back while Libby helped her on with her winter coat. A lamp on the ottoman which Libby had clicked into life gave the line of the girl's body in the angora dress an aurora of peach-coloured fire.

The baize door had once marked the boundary of the servants' quarters; kitchen, scullery and morning room. You could still see a box on the kitchen wall to which bells serving various parts of the house had been connected. There were no servants now; just Mrs Armitage, a not-particularly-nice old thing who came in three days a week to do light cleaning, to leave copies of *The Watchtower* lying around and to harangue Libby about the Great Darwin Fraud (Mrs Armitage was a Jehovah's

Witness). Libby did everything else herself, always had done, including cooking our meals at the huge coal–fired range, which needed constant stoking and attending. She often complained about this – but tonight she was silent as she warmed a can of Heinz tomato soup for Amy and me. Seated at the kitchen table, pretending to read the instructions printed on my new packet of Bics, I watched for a lightening of her mood.

'Where's the shaving foam?' I asked eventually.

'In the downstairs lavatory.'

'Have we got a streptic...?

'Styptic pencil? No. They don't work anyway: use tissue paper if you cut yourself.' She never said *toilet* paper, or even *lavatory* paper; always *tissue*, the tees and esses rustling like expensive presents.

'Perhaps I ought to cut my tongue out.'

'Don't be gruesome.' She went upstairs with a tray for Amy.

'Aren't you having anything?' I asked when she came back.

'Not for me. Bath and an early night. Switch off after you.'

'Libby, what was all that in the high street about?'

She swallowed rather suddenly then left the room with a murmured goodnight.

The downstairs lavatory opened off the morning room. Two steps took you down into a space under the stairs where tennis rackets came when they died, where a rusted épée of Martin's hinted at a dashing sporting past, and where our ski boots had lived ever since the family stopped going on winter holidays. I found the can of shaving foam in the cupboard underneath the tiny basin, ran the taps and squooshed some out into my palm.

The cuts started almost immediately – my anxious, blood-streaked face in the mirror, her bath running in the pipes. I thought about the sound her new shoes had made, following her home down Cato Road: the faint squelch of delicate soles. I thought about the gap between us as we'd filed down the path. Normally we'd be huddled together between the cypresses, she'd be chattering in my ear…I would smell Mitsouko, face powder and a honeyed musk of breath. I felt widening panic, ripples of unease spreading outwards into darkness. Mum was never usually the word.

'What on earth did he say to get Boy so riled?'

The kitchen stilled.

Libby replied in a tobacco-furred voice, 'My God, Clem, if I'd *known* what that silly piece of gossip was going to put me through…!' She glanced towards the far end of the table where I was sitting, then buried her face in her hands. 'Why was I born so horrible?' The candle flames moved. 'Such a terrible mother!' They flared out sideways, guttering under the growing onslaught of male laughter. 'I shouldn't be allowed – why am I just this awful BITCH?'

Cracker litter scuttled over the table edge in fright. I sat tranced with indignation. It wasn't unusual for Libby and me to have different recollections of things, hers usually funnier – but this was a travesty. I felt as if someone had just smacked me in the face. Which in a way she had.

Up until now I'd been enjoying the show. There was the story of her recent humiliation in our local paper shop; the Freudian parapraxis that had caused her to mangle the title of the magazine she was asking for so that it came out as *Harpers and Queer* (the newsagent was gay). 'Do you take *Homos and Gardens* too?' had chortled Robin Butler, my art master, and I'd felt flattered to be included in the joke. Along with the goose had come some chestnuts – Mrs Price's Wig, the Three Gold Chairs – all tales told against herself, all featuring that familiar self-deprecating ostinato: *I'm so terrible, I'm so bad, I shouldn't be allowed*... It was Libby's style to make herself, ostensibly at least, the butt.

'But that's not the worst of it... Listen to what happened in the high street yesterday...' I was still wiping tears of laughter from my eyes at this point, careful not to dislodge the bloodied bits of bog paper stuck all over my chin. As the story unfolded, through her whitewash, her producer's rewrite, I felt the impotent rage of a Winston Smith boiling in my veins. It wasn't like that, I wanted to scream in their laughing faces as she described Boy's fury; it hadn't happened that way at all.

But they were so epileptic with mirth that they wouldn't even have noticed. Pawing the table. Eating their napkins. 'What the hell did he *say*?'

'He just happened to mention Lilith's unfortunate little accident.' Libby got up to collect the pudding plates and the laughter gently subsided, male eyes following her hips as they circled the kitchen table.

What story *was* this, exactly, dear?' said Mrs Parks. Evidently Imelda, not really one of the inner circle (being a woman and Libby preferring men), hadn't been treated to this particular piece of gossip.

'Oh, you know, darling,' said Libby with an impatient gesture. 'The one about Lilith setting fire to her bedroom.'

'I hadn't heard.'

15

'Yes, she's back on the sauce again. Luckily they're right next door to a fire station. Good job, because the place is an absolute fire trap—' dumping the plates on the dishwasher, she dropped heavily into her place at Robin's side and reached for her cigarettes. 'Have you *seen* the place?' Robin nodded, giggling. '*So* bloody nouveau: everything ruched and swagged and shagged to buggery. No wonder it went up so fast, imagine: you can just see the candlewick bedspread catching the broderie anglaise valance, the valance catching the Afghan rug; the rug catching the swirly carpet, the carpet the curtains – shantung, hideous – and before you know it…Match me, Robin.' Red-eyed with laughing, Robin struck a Swan Vesta. 'It's a mercy really. Except that the redecoration, from what I've heard, is ten times worse.'

Mrs Parks, who had begun to take mental inventory of her own soft furnishings, suddenly showed all the gaiety of faded upholstery. 'But was Lilith hurt?'

'Just a moderate singeing,' breathed Libby.

'And that was what set him off, was it,' said Clem Arnos, our solicitor, 'that silly little story about the fire?' The hubbub around the kitchen table dipped abruptly.

Her Safe Pair of Hands, Libby called Clem (he kept goal for a team in the Isthmian league). I could vouch for the literal truth of this backhanded compliment, having watched him field Amy inches from the floor when illness and fatigue had toppled her from her chair. But tonight there was an edge to him. 'There must have been more to it than that, surely?'

'Come off it,' said Robin. 'How would you feel if someone accused your mother of setting fire to the house in an alcoholic stupor?'

'He never said she'd been drinking. Did you, Harry?'

Eyes around the table turned my way, sallow with boozy mirth.

'No.'

'You see?' said Clem. 'The drink problem wasn't even mentioned.' The gaze was impassive in the sandy face, but I noticed that neither Robin nor Libby met it.

'Oh, don't be so bloody...jurisprudential,' she said.

Clem was insistent. 'That story's common knowledge.'

'Everybody knows,' I chipped in.

'Everybody knows,' cried Libby. 'Exactly what he said to Boy! Everybody knows!'

'Everybody knows!' chorused the grown-ups to each other — all except for Clem, who shook his head hopelessly.

'Let Truth go naked, why not?' laughed the priest.

'Why not?' smiled Robin, uneasily.

'It's a fair point,' said Councillor Parks (Cyril Parks-and-Amenities). 'Everybody *does* know—' he glanced at his wife '—more or less...'

'Exactly,' said Clem, stabbing his words into the table-cloth with a squat finger. 'What the *hell* was there to *get* so up-*set* about?'

'Oh, come on Clem,' said Libby. 'You get hold of a thing and you worry away at it like a dog with an old shoe...Boy's the school toughie at Wentworth—'

'Practically runs the place,' Robin rushed to confirm.

'And this little fifth-former, a new boy, comes up and tells him that it's common knowledge his mother leapt naked onto a fireman's back—'

'She didn't!' hissed Imelda, scandalized.

'—Of course he's going to go spare.'

'What do *you* think, Harry?' said Clem, his chair

17

creaking as he turned. 'How did it seem to you?'

Libby's eyes, over the ice buckets choked with dead-men, flashed me a warning. 'Harry remembers just what I remember,' she snapped. 'Neither of us will ever forget it.' She screwed her cigarette into the ashtray.

'Why, though,' persisted Clem, 'why your mother rather than you, eh?'

'Me organ-grinder, Hal monkey.'

'No, Libby.' Clem was trenchant. 'There's something you're not telling us, and I can see from Harry's face too...'

'Look, for God's sake, Clem—' said the councillor.

'—Yes, give it a rest, Clem,' said Robin. 'It's Christmas and all.'

'Just *look* at the poor boy,' said Imelda Parks, making a ghastly poor-puppy moue in my direction.

Clem opened his mouth to say something, then thought better of it. I watched as he stroked his ginger moustache and examined the lees of his wine.

'I'm just a terrible mother!' wailed Libby, to break the silence.

'We all make terrible mistakes when we bring up children,' Councillor Parks said ruefully, adjusting the waistband of his trousers: '*They fuck you up, your mum and dad*—'

'*Please*, Cyril!' snapped his wife, then turned her spaniel eyes on me again. I had a strong urge to punch her.

'It's all my fault,' moaned Libby, 'I taught him how to speak—'

'The gift of language!' nodded the priest.

'—Exactly, you give them the gift of language, and this is how they repay you.'

I stared at the napkin in my lap, a stained twist of damask.

'He's growing up all gossipy, like a woman. Not enough male influence – Martin away all the time. Oh, if only I were a good person but I'm not. I'm bad. Evil people like me oughtn't to be *allowed* to have children . . .'

'Dear dear Libby!' exclaimed Father Malachi, placing an arm lightly around her shoulders, stealing a glance at his watch as he did so. 'You're a wonderful mother and you've two of the finest children – where *is* the head of the household, by the way? still over there with those fearful Germans, is he . . . ?'

'Just look at the lad!' cooed Mrs Parks.

'Face like a smacked arse,' agreed Cyril, swallowing a belch.

After that I remember Libby coming towards me at the foot of the stairs, puckering up for a goodnight kiss. O the hard dark lustre of those eyes. That's the way I am, they seemed to say – bad. *Shouldn't be allowed . . . But you can't help forgiving me, can you?*

'You're a fuckin' cow, mother.' Already she was turning away with her clanking armful of spirit bottles towards the sound of a fracas developing in the sitting room, where the guests had retired after Father Malachi had left to read midnight mass.

I remember the spaces of the stairwell in swirling motion, a dark weight of air pressing down. I remember the sound of voices raised and bodies falling. A distant crack of sundering wood.

III

That Christmas morning neither of us exactly threw back our sheets barking like dogs to be let at the day. I was woken well past nine by the faint knocking of a pipe as Libby ran water in her room.

Amy must have heard it too; soon she came padding down from the attic and after a fraught negotiation on the landing, Libby's side of which was too muffled to make out, her sickly little face appeared around my door.

'Mummy's not well.'

'She'll get over it.'

Amy coughed, then shivered. 'What about Presents?'

'Presents after Breakfast.'

She thought about this for a moment, then suggested I make breakfast. It seemed too difficult to explain that this wouldn't bring Presents along any faster. 'Just go back to bed.'

Eventually there was the sound of scuttle and tongs rattling through the plumbing, a bacon smell creeping up the stairs. I went down to find Libby in her dressing gown with fish-slice in one hand and Alka-Seltzer in the other. This morning her skin had a slightly waxy look. A lattice of fine lines was visible where the light caught the cheekbone.

'I don't want egg and bacon, I only want cereal,' Amy was saying.

'Have whatever you like, darling,' said her mother. 'It's Christmas . . . How about you, grumpy Hal? An egg? Have two.' The plate arrived in front of me bearing two eggs and an extra share of bacon.

I picked up my knife and fork and began to eat, while Libby, warming herself against the range, chewed speculatively on a slice of dry toast. She looked old this morning, I told myself, ignoring the fact that she also looked good. Even with her hair unbrushed and no make-up.

'Cheer up, Hal. It might never happen.'

Amy watched us severely over her empty cereal bowl. Not much trouble guessing what was concentrating my sister's tight little features. A huge doll's house, Clem and Robin's joint gift, had sat under the tree for a week now, too huge to disguise with wrapping paper, the constant sight of it driving the five-year-old slowly into a frenzy of impatience. When breakfast was cleared Libby spoke the word – Presents – that sent her springing like a greyhound from the trap, bashing through the green baize door into the hall. We caught up with her in the sitting room. Amy had come to an abrupt halt, surveying on the carpet in front of her a mess of wood shards held together with shreds of miniature wallpaper, a litter of scattered tiny furniture.

'Oh dear,' said Libby, 'I'd forgotten about—'

I put an arm around my little sister, who was clutching a doll-sized loo in her fist and staring blankly at the tree, hardly seeing the coloured bulbs, the wisps of angel hair.

It would have taken more than a smashed doll's house to derail a Housemartin Christmas. Once under way there was no stopping the thing: Church followed Presents and with iron logic Pub followed Church.

Three Bloody Marys in the Smack bucked Libby up no end. Her acolytes had looked a sorry sight shuffling in the door, eyeing the optics warily as they hung up their coats; but with their leader throwing out the old riffs, cutting deep into that self-flagellating groove – *God, I'm such an old soak* – things were soon in full swing.

I watched the escalating bonhomie from the children's room in the company of Amy and a horde of screaming over-hyped-up kids: a bottle of Coke (with straws!) in front of me, my hand in a greasy packet of crisps. Towards closing time the Christmas spirit really began to take hold in the saloon bar; even Robin and Clem were smiling and slapping each other's back like the best of friends – though the bandage on Clem's wrist impeded his slapping somewhat, and Robin's smile looked a bit skew-whiff on account of a black eye. Inevitably there was a spat over which one of them should drive us home, Robin looking demolished when Libby opted for Clem's Rover. 'Let me take one of you, at least,' he pleaded, trailing Libby across the carpark then, realizing the idiocy of what he had said, adding,

'You, Harry, you'd like a spin in the Dyane, wouldn't you?'

More in the vague hope of annoying Libby than anything else, I accepted.

'We'll go the Pretty Way,' he said, looking a little surprised when the engine started first time. The Citroën smelled rank, bunged up with canvases, easels and other art essentials (mainly empty beer cans). 'So, Martin's taken the car, has he? That's a bit steep.'

I stared incredulously. 'Libby can't drive. She failed her test, remember? You were at the commiseration party.'

'Yes, of course.'

The Pretty Way avoided the one-in-six hill that was the direct route out of the old town, the route Clem had taken. Instead it snaked up the cliffs, giving a view over the estuary. Robin swung off the road near the top and parked. 'Look at that,' he said, waving his arm with cramped extravagance. 'Beautiful.'

The tide was out. Despite a lone shaft of sunlight piercing the clouds over Canvey to spotlight the chimneys of the refinery, the vista looked sodden and glum.

'Don't seem your usual self today, Harry.'

'You were there last night.'

'What's the matter – can't take a bit of ribbing?'

The wind whistled eerily in his broken sunroof.

'Come on, you've got a wonderful relationship with your mother, you know you have. I hardly ever met mine, I was brought up by nannies.'

Robin was the third son of a baronet, though he smoked roll-ups, lived in squalor and belonged to the Socialist Workers' Party; all entirely risible in Clem's view

– Clem of the authentically flat northern A, whose father had bathed in a tin bath in front of the fire and who was now treasurer of the local Conservative Association.

'And you're lucky she's so young, so good-looking.'

'What difference does it make to me what she looks like? She's my mother.'

He rumpled his dark locks. 'I don't know, it just does, doesn't it? When you have to see them every morning over the cornflakes? The way people look makes a difference. Shouldn't, I suppose, but it does.' He gazed across the mud towards the power station on the Isle of Grain. 'Not enough Beauty in the world.' After a long pause, during which I was conscious principally of the cold draught blowing up one leg of my jeans, he said, 'I ought to get you back.'

This time it took several goes to start the engine.

For all the fuss Libby made about carving the bird and torching the pudding with vodka, she hardly ate a thing at dinner. Her laughter was shrill as she read out the jokes from the crackers. 'What's round and bad-tempered?' 'A vicious circle.' 'Arf 'arf.

Nervous jollity couldn't disguise the truth, which was that a bad atmosphere, compound of our various grievances, had settled over the table.

'For God's sake, somebody *else* say something,' she cried at last, dropping the spoon onto her pudding plate.

Amy coughed and said weakly, 'Mummy, when can we get my doll's house fixed?'

'Very soon.'

'Can we do it before Daddy comes back, so it looks nice for him?'

Libby pushed her plate aside and lit a cigarette. 'I doubt that he would notice, sweetheart.'

I cleared my throat, 'You should get Clem to fix it, looks like he's pretty good with his hands.'

Libby just glared at me then looked away.

After lunch we had a fire in the sitting room and played Scrabble, Libby hugging her knees and bending forward on the sofa, while Amy made patterns on the Axminster with a pack of paisley-backed cards. *The Queen of Hearts, she made some tarts, all on a summer's day,* sang Amy. Suddenly she clutched herself between the legs.

'Do you want a wee-wee, darling?' said Libby. Amy nodded.

'Run upstairs.'

Her thin legs disappeared around the door.

'Nipple' was on the rack in front of me. I had just noticed that I could get both 'lip' and 'pen' out of it when Libby said quietly, 'How long is this going to go on?'

'This?'

Tongues of flames danced on the whites of her eyes. 'It's not very friendly, is it – at Christmas? What am I supposed to have done, Hal?' On the TV screen, blood pulsed through a vein in section. 'You're being very childish.'

'I *am* a child, remember? When it suits you.' Too old to be sitting on the floor, I squirmed with discomfort.

'What does that mean?' The fire crackled. 'If it's about last night then I'm sorry if you can't take a joke. At least now you know how it feels to be humiliated in public like that. Can't we just say that we're even and make up?'

'Even?'

'Yes, darling, even. Deep and crisp and even.' She smoothed her skirt.

'What I did in the high street was accidental. What you did last night was deliberate. That's one nil down in my book, not even.'

'Just Mummy getting her own back.'

'You went out of your way to hurt me.'

'Don't take it so seriously.' She giggled and leant forwards, her chin on her knees.

I looked at her then looked quickly away. 'It felt serious.'

'That's the way the world is, Hal. You do things that are wrong and you don't realize until too late. And sometimes you don't even know *why* they're wrong...'

'Well, that's very profound. So you were teaching me a zen lesson, were you?'

'No, Hal, I—'

'No, that wasn't it, was it? It was another kind of lesson: this is how bad I can make things for you if you poke your nose in—'

'Hal—!'

'—So that I would think twice before I decided to start blabbing off about it; like, for instance, how strange it was that Boy should get so angry at you, when it was me that blurted out about Lilith and her fag butt. Why was *that*? And what did he mean by calling you a *lying slag*?'

She crossed her legs and reached for her cigarettes. 'I didn't understand what he was on about any more than you did. He's completely bonkers; it's that mother of his...'

'What about her?'

'Let's not go into that.'

'It's all right; you can trust me. I've learnt my lesson.'

26

'So have I. That's why I'm not telling you.'

'Telling me what?'

'Nothing. Forget it. There's nothing to tell.'

Blood surged through the valves, platelets tumbled. I shifted my position again.

'Look,' she relented, 'I'm sorry. But you know what a terrible person I am...'

'Here we go: I'm so bad, I'm so awful...It's just something you say; it doesn't mean anything.'

'Do you want me to beg, Hal? Forgive me now! Stop being so bloody self-righteous.'

She fumbled with her cigarette packet for a while before tossing it aside. 'Hal,' she said, holding her arms out, laughing. 'Look at me. I've said I'm sorry, now. Please?' Her perfume wafted in my direction. 'For God's sake?' She smiled and tucked her legs under her on the sofa, kicking her shoes away as she did so. Coltishly. She had coltish calves, that's what Robin had said about her at some point the previous night. Coltish – the word kept repeating in my head as I stared at her legs... Coltish... Then, with a blush, I focused on the shoes she had kicked away instead. Their soles slightly corrugated, coming loose; their delicate black suede uppers showing a faint salt stain...

'Stop staring at my shoes, you come here and give me a hug.'

The room felt too hot suddenly, my clothes too tight. The platelets pile in then try to back out again, but the valve snaps shut. Her arms were still held out, her calves tucked under her thighs (O the hard lustre of those thighs). Somewhere beneath my diaphragm a weak ache was beginning. An uncontrollable forcing forward. I

27

looked at her and the trapped blood pulsed. *Jesus wept.*

'Hal,' she said, catching the look of panic in my face. 'Is something wrong?'

Amy was blocking the stairs: 'I've done wee in my knickers,' she said. I shoved past her and she ran crying to Libby. 'Harry pushed me and said pissoff,' her voice carolled up the dark vault of the stairwell. 'He shouldn't do that, Mummy, should he?'

'No, darling, he shouldn't,' came Libby's muffled tones.

Safe behind the locked door of my bedroom I cooled my face against the window pane. In the garden, snow lay around in hard, isolated hillocks under a sky the colour of weak tea. I opened the window wide and went and sat on the bed, then picked up a book and snapped on the clock radio. I read the same page over and over without taking it in, until the cold crept up on me and the erection gradually subsided.

IV

'Why don't you love our mummy any more?' asked my sister as we walked in the park zoo on Boxing Day.

'Because she's a bitch.'

'She's not, she's a lovely mummy.' Amy stopped in front of the largest of the cages and narrowed her eyes at the sad bundle of fur slumped in its corner. 'Poor Willie.' Willie was the zoo's star attraction. As far as I could see, Willie had two modes, functionally indistinguishable: basking, for when the sun was out, sulking, for when it wasn't. 'It's because he hasn't got anyone to play with, that's why he looks sad. There ought to be a girl bear.'

'No room in the cage,' I said absently, distracted by cries from the football field.

Suddenly Amy began to cough violently, beating her hands against her chest.

'Here,' said a familiar voice behind me. Amy's eyes lit

up. I turned to see Anne Singleton and her dog. Nipper had a new tartan collar and lead. His mistress was wearing a boy's denim jacket, from the pocket of which she had plucked a small white handkerchief embroidered with blue flowers. Her brief, contemptuous glance told me that we were still where we'd left off in the hall before Christmas. Who but an idiot adolescent male, it seemed to say, would take sickly Amy out without a hand-kerchief?

'Hi, Anne, is that Colin's jacket?'

The remark didn't unsettle her as much as I'd hoped. It didn't unsettle her at all. With an impatient click of the tongue she transferred her attention straight to Amy. 'How's the 'flu?'

'I've got a nasty cough now as well,' said Amy, demonstrating with the help of the handkerchief. Hearing it through Anne's ears, it sounded ominous; a grown-up's forty-a-day rumble and hawk coming from a frail five-year-old body. Anne glared her concern at me. 'That *is* a nasty cough.' Crouching, closing Amy's fingers around the handkerchief, she was tender: 'You can borrow it until you're better.' But when she straightened up and turned to me the smile had cooled. 'Don't keep her out too long.'

I watched the easy sway of her hips as she walked away, Nipper straining after a poodle turd but getting no slack. Girls always know when you're looking at their bottoms. In this case, you could tell, the knowledge occasioned no nerves.

'Let's go and watch the football,' I said.

Amy coughed most of the way to the football field, where two teams of men in coloured strips were shouting urgent syllables. 'To me, Mal' – 'Man on, Tel.'

'Isn't that Uncle Clem in goal?' she spluttered.

'He's not your uncle.'

'But is it?'

'Looks like him.'

Suddenly a yet more violent spasm seized her. Pity vied with irritation at the sight of those pale cheeks puffed out like a jazz trumpeter's – blowing a solo that seemed as if it was never going to end. I helped her to a seat in the nearby shelter and we sat it out together.

'Are you all right?' I said at last.

'I think so.'

'Wait here a minute. I just want a word with Clem.'

I walked over to the goalpost and called 'Hi' through the side netting. Clem was swaying rhythmically from foot to foot, safe hands sheathed in mud-encrusted gloves. 'Something up with Amy?' he said, eyes fixed on the far end of the field.

'Just a bit of a cough. What's the score?'

'One nil down.'

'I wanted a word about Christmas Eve.'

'The doll's house, eh? Robin fell over on it.' A sidelong look. 'Okay, I took a poke at him and knocked him over. He leaves it to me to buy the thing then complains I've overspent. Typical bloody socialist: generous with everybody's money but his own—'

'It wasn't the doll's house I wanted to talk about, actually...' I gave him my version of the encounter with Boy Hugg in the high street, explaining how far Libby had wandered from the truth. '... You were right to pick her up on it, Clem, there's something more there...'

He looked grave, serious breath frosting the air. 'I was

31

a bit drunk that night, Harry—'

'—And why would he call her a *lying slag*? What's going on? She won't tell me a thing.'

'Look here, Harry.' A hand moved to his moustache. 'It's not easy for Libby, you know, with Martin away all the time, paying the bills on that big place. You oughtn't to—'

Suddenly the ground trembled. The thud of booted feet against earth came our way. An opposing forward had broken, chased by three backs. Clem spat, crouched and started shouting. He went out to narrow the angle, but the shot never came; just inside the box, one of the backs swiped the attacker's legs from under him.

A whistle blew.

I looked over to where Amy was sitting; breath steamed from the hot little mouth in gusts. When I turned back Clem was crouched to face the penalty. You could sense the tension in his thighs (while Amy's distant bark fretted at some corner of my attention).

'Uncle Clem didn't stop the ball,' she said when I went back to fetch her. 'Does that mean it's a goal?'

'Let's go home.' I felt depressed. The grown-ups were closing ranks.

'Can I ask you something, Hal?'

'Fire away.'

I was expecting the girl questions: 'What's offside?' or 'Why do they eat oranges at half-time?' Instead she unbunched her little fist and showed me what was in her handkerchief: a glob of mucus veined with blood, livid against the white cotton with its tiny blue flowers.

'Is that bad?'

V

There was always something not quite right about Amy.

I remember Libby's nails cutting into my arm, night-gown wet between the legs, the bedroom floor awash with amniotic fluid and tea: she'd been delivering a morning cuppa when her waters broke and she started delivering Amy instead. Two months early.

I didn't actually see my precipitate new sister until a couple of days later in the hospital. They had her under a sun lamp in a Perspex box, a twist of parchment held by a tiny plastic clamp marking the severed point of connection. She looked scrunched and blue, no bigger than a rat.

'Yuk,' I said.

'Don't be like that,' said Libby. 'The poor little wibblet's fighting for her life. What shall we call her?'

'You mean you haven't got a name?'

'Not yet. I thought I'd wait until . . .' She didn't finish the sentence.

Libby's God was an Indian giver. It had a slightly chilling side to it, this attitude, showing up in small things. I'd had my Cash's name-tapes from birth. Amy's were left until the very last minute.

Next morning I was woken by a conversation starting up outside my door and followed the voices out onto the landing. Libby's sounded unusually shrill. 'I've given her Aconite, Doctor.'

The mottled face of our GP registered amusement. 'Aco——?'

'Aconite: a homoeopathic remedy for diseases of the chest.'

'Of course. Homoeopathy.' Porcine eyes, too closely grouped around his razor-thin nose, kept wandering towards her own chest. 'Used to work in a dispensary, didn't you? Well, it probably won't do any harm; by all means carry on if you wish – just don't neglect the penicillin.' He gestured at the scrap of paper she was clutching with white fingers.

'But is that all——? The blood: she's bringing up blood!'

'I wouldn't worry too much about the haemoptysis. It's all that coughing, bit of tearing of the lung maybe. Nothing to worry about unduly.'

'Haemo . . . ?'

I followed them down. On the mat Libby accepted a grave-marked hand whose touch, experience told me, was ice. 'Penicillin,' he urged, 'that's the stuff.'

Libby lingered on the threshold for a while after he'd gone, blinking absently at the cypresses. 'Clear the snow off the path can you, Hal; we don't want Mrs Armitage getting a greenstick fracture or something.' By the sound of it, she'd been up all night with her medical dictionary. 'You don't think it's my fault, do you?' In microscope vision I watched the cold air from the open door raise tiny hairs on the side of her neck, puckering skin into goose bumps. Shoulders drooped. 'Oh, why did I let her stay up so late on Christmas Eve—?' Suddenly she spun around. 'Come here and give your mother a hug, Hal ... Hal? What's the matter? Why are you looking at me like that?'

I dropped my eyes, fixing on the pattern of the parquet flooring.

Maybe, I thought as I cleared the path, shovel rasping and then dinging against the edge of uneven stones, there were nodal points in time where reality forked, parallel universes. In one of these universes I'd chosen to buttonhole Boy. In another I hadn't. Somehow I'd got stuck in the wrong one.

Snow shucked by the cypresses fell on my back. I worked feverishly, cursing the irregular tilt of the stones. The shovel scraped, struck sparks on the stones, bit moss where it grew proud of the interstices. You only had to look at that eruption in the sitting room (the heat of the room to blame, surely – or hormones out of sync).

Fresh snow fell. Absorption in the task increased. It seemed important, somehow, deadly important, to clear every stone. The honed blade came up gleaming at the edge now. Rolls of moss scratched out and kicked towards the shrubbery were strewn along the path's edge. At some point realization dawned that for the last half an hour I'd been clearing solely fresh snow.

The shovel fell with a clang.

'What have you been *doing* all day?' said Libby, sitting heavily on the end of my bed, 'I've hardly seen you.'

I let the book flop over my crotch.

She glanced at the cover. '*Three Towers at Treblinka?*'

'It's about the Death Camps.'

'How can you read in the dark?' She got up and clicked on the overhead light, then walked over to draw the curtains. 'And with the window open – aren't you freezing?'

'I felt hot.'

She tutted. 'Well, why not just turn the radiator down?' – Bending to adjust the valve, stretching skirt material – 'Buggeration, how do you work these things?'

'Don't . . . Don't fuss. I'll do it myself, Libby, just leave me alone.'

'What's the matter, Hal?'

'Nothing. Leave me alone.'

I couldn't avoid her forever. Helpless as any other young middle-class male when it came to domestic functions – food, washing, ironing (how the fuck did you do that?) – I had to live. Mealtimes, in particular, had to be got through.

That evening I took *Three Towers at Treblinka* down to dinner. Walking skeletons, lampshades of human skin. Just the job. But when it came time for the clearing of the plates I heard a clatter of crockery and looked up to see Libby advancing on me, eyes streaming, mascara-smeared cheeks aglow, the hot woman smell rising between us.

'Hal, you win, I can't take it any longer. If it's really the thing in the high street that's bothering you so much, okay, we'll talk about it... But you've got to meet me halfway.'

She halted, took a deep, bosom-inflating breath and held out her arms.

Perhaps my mother was just one of those women – Mailer's Marilyn, Wedekind's Lulu – to whose chemical potency no reagent male, not even a blood relative, could long remain immune.

'Come on, Hal, it's got to be worth a *hug*!'

Suddenly she froze and a hand flew to her mouth. I tracked her eyeline to the window where a shape, a shadow among shadows, was falling off the edge of my vision.

Slippered feet broke the crust of snow as I rounded the house, following the beam of a torch grabbed on my way through the scullery. I came to a halt among frosted skeletons of apple trees, torch beam swinging from trunk to trunk, from branch to snow-thickened branch.

The threat from the prowler seemed as nothing compared to the dangerous emotions attached to that body in the kitchen, whose anxious face I could see now, shadowed by the single overhead bulb; though being outside the circle of light it threw into the orchard I was pretty certain she couldn't see me. Under cover of darkness I adjusted my underpants.

Swinging the torch around under the kitchen window, my beam fell on the print of an AirWair sole, Greek cross emblazoning the instep – so fresh that you could read its mirror-writing litany of resistances: oil, alkali, petrol.

'Who was it, Libby?'

'How should *I* know?'

'You saw him.'

'Not properly.'

'You said, "It's him" or something.'

'Did I? I thought I just sort of gasped.'

'Oh, come *on*.'

'Don't bully me, Hal.'

I looked at her closely. 'Libby, who was it?'

In the silence a name formed which neither of us had the courage, or perhaps the bad taste, to acknowledge.

Salt

I

Somehow we kept expecting Amy to get better, somehow she didn't. Over the next couple of weeks her nightly concerto of coughing swelled to a regular five-movement symphony with terrifying sforzandos of hawk, rack and retch. Libby's increasingly frequent trips up the attic stairs were punctuated by frantic calls to Dr Summerbee, from whom I guessed that she was getting no slack, because the night before I went back to school I heard her on the phone to Germany – where Martin had spent Christmas as the guest of his business associate, Franz Lammergeier – voice rising steadily in pitch and volume. 'He won't even make a house call, he's got it into his head that it's just a chest infection when anyone in their right mind can see it must be at *least* pneumonia... For God's sake, Martin, come home; she's your daughter too...' Then a pause. Then a thud and tinkle as the receiver was slammed down.

Next morning at breakfast she looked fucked. Her fingers trembled under the weight of the teapot.

'Amy's not going to school this morning then,' I said. She gawked in mock surprise at being spoken to.

'And have you stopped eating or something? Won't do her any good if *you* get ill.'

'My God, conversation – thank you very much for your concern, but I had a doughnut earlier.'

'A doughnut's not much.'

'Rubbish. I practically lived on them when I was breast-feeding you...Remember?' Unfortunately I did. At the age of five and she had still been whipping them out on demand. 'Didn't stop me going from thirty-six C to double D in a month—'

'I think that's the door.'

Clem stood in the porch. 'I've come for Amy's doll's house. Thought it might cheer her up a bit if I got it fixed.'

I led him down the passageway, noticing Libby as we entered the kitchen prepare a face, smooth hands over her sweater-front.

'Robin's taking care of that,' she protested when Clem explained.

'The Road to Hell is paved with things Robin said he'd take care of,' drawled Clem.

Together he and I retrieved the sad bundle of shivered plywood from the garage and loaded it into the boot of his Rover. 'Lift to school?'

When I returned to the house for my satchel Libby was waiting with a book she'd borrowed from Robin over the holidays. 'Better give this back – I won't bother to ask for a goodbye kiss.'

*

The still-warm car interior smelled sexily of leather. A local station came on with the ignition. We slid out into Cato Road, motor sighing contemptuously at the gradient, the Carpenters oozing out of the stereo.

'Power steering?'

'Comes as standard.'

Clem put a foot to the floor and I watched his sure grip on the wheel, his deft flick of the indicator, over-taking a slower, less gleaming car.

Eventually he reached out and silenced Karen Carpenter – 'I won't last a day without' click. 'She's desperate to make it up, you know, Harry.'

'Oh?'

During the previous fortnight my relationship with my mother had settled into something closer to the accepted norm. If she walked into a room, I generally walked out of it.

'But it's hard when you won't let her know what she's supposed to have done.'

A whip-thin Anne Singleton flashed past my window pinned to a hedge by Colin Garganey, her gaze locking momentarily with mine, wall-eyed indifference veined with feminine contempt. 'I think she's got a fair idea.'

'That thing in the high street? You're not still holding that against her, are you?'

'All I want to know is why Boy seems to hate her so much.'

Lashless eyelids narrowed at the road ahead. 'Well, now that you're both back at school, why don't you ask him?'

I almost gagged on my stupefied laughter.

'Best to tackle these things head on, don't you think? Take the bull by the *cojones*?'

'You're seriously suggesting I try and talk to Boy again after what happened last time?' I shook my head in disbelief.

'Why not, if you can't get anything out of Libby? Not that I'm necessarily implying there *is* anything to get out of Libby.' There was a creak of leather upholstery as Clem shifted nervously in his seat.

'Of course not.'

Clem clicked the radio back on, signalling End of Conversation. For the rest of the trip I contemplated the drear uniformity of suburban flora: weeping willow, monkey-puzzle, plane, chestnut . . .

'Gray?'

'Present.'

'Grey?'

'Present.'

'Haase?'

'Present.'

'Housemartin—' Not the usual dawn chorus at the mention of my risible surname today. Instead, a low funeral humming.

'Housemartin?' insisted my form master, Cowley, crossly.

'Present,' I said.

'So what was that all about?' he asked me when the classroom had cleared and he had beckoned me over. 'Singing you the Death March?'

'Don't know, sir.'

'Sure? Someone picking on you?' He eyed me sceptically over the miniature snowdrifts of scurf that settled in his rims. 'We don't tolerate bullying in this school.' He sounded as if he were reading out of the prospectus.

'Don't know, sir.'

'*Omertà*, eh?'

'I beg your pardon?'

'Oh Myrrh Tar: the Mafia code of silence – good God, Housemartin, don't you go to the pictures?'

Something was definitely up. I'd noticed it walking into the yard first thing, the sidelong looks and clucking tongues that usually registered with merciless exactness the value of my stock showing a lower value, if possible, than ever. Your stock is fucked.

Malcolm Finch had ambled over, polishing his glasses: 'How's your mother, Housemartin?' he squinted at me, 'Got over her nasty experience in the high street yet?'

I stared at a notch on the bridge of his nose that could have been put there by Evolution. 'Who told you?'

'Chrissie.' Boy's younger brother.

'What would it be worth to keep it to yourself?'

Malcolm gave me a withering look and replaced his glasses. 'Everybody knows, Harry.'

'Unbelievable,' I complained as we filed into assembly together. 'All this fuss just because his mother has an accident with a fag butt.'

'Accident. She downs a bottle of Mogadon and torches the bed with her best onyx table lighter: doesn't sound much like an accident to me.' The eyes were categorical behind their lenses. 'By the way, did you really say that to Boy: that it must have been a shock to wake up and find her bed alight?' He chuckled mirthlessly. 'Nice one, Harry.'

Boy was still there up on stage, to the right of the

45

headmaster's lectern, gleaming Doc Martens planted four-square on the boards in front of him. No one seemed able to explain this, given that his predecessor, Foxcroft, was now back at school, hobbling around on crutches with the cowed look of a headshy dog and a brand-new Arthur Mullard profile.

I watched Boy scanning the knowing faces ranged before him like a light gun reading bar codes. From time to time he would chance across somebody he knew and a wolfish grin would split the mask. Then it was back to the scanning, the efficient little flick of the eye at the end of each row, as if he were looking for one face in particular.

Cowley had given me a book that he had borrowed to return to Robin in the art block. It was first break before I managed to get down that way.

Art One was light, high-ceilinged and as malodorous in its own way as Robin's Dyane, smelling of wet clay and the diseased elm logs he got his first years to draw. Robin was alone at his desk, marking. As I handed over the book he looked up, mouth crimped with silent laughter, and handed me in return one of the pencil drawings from a large pile in front of him. 'This ought to interest you, Harry.'

Harsh adolescent laughter came from the little back room whose open doorway stood about three yards behind his left shoulder. Once, when Arts One and Two were the school dining hall, this room had been a kitchen. Now it was Sixth Form Art. The A level art students warmed themselves at its still-functioning oven on winter mornings, lighting the gas with spills torn from younger boys' work and generally larking about. As I watched, a thin stream of red liquid shot across the empty doorway, and a voice that I instantly recognized as Boy's brayed, '*Pe*ckinpah!'

'Keep the noise down in there!' shouted Robin, ineffectually.

The drawing was of a middle-aged woman, her face seemingly put together out of discrete joints of some boneless white meat, depending from invisible hooks under a harsher gravity than earth's. Careful hatching charted the fall of a strangely lunar light over jowl and dewlap, every clotted wrinkle, every shattered vein noted with a pathologist's unshirking eye. 'Ugly.'

'Magnificently ugly. How's *your* mother, by the way?'

I looked up, suspicious. 'Why, whose mother is this?'

'Guess.' He was brimming with amusement. 'Getting on any better yet, Libby and you?'

'No.'

'You really ought to try and make it up with her, you know.' He tried to look severe but the smile kept breaking out, fitfully corrugating his long upper lip. 'Still don't get it? Read the inscription. It's an illustration exercise you see — illustrate a quotation from the bible.'

Neatly lettered, on a little quattrocento scroll: *As newborn babes desire the sincere milk of the Word.*

'Odd choice of model if you ask me... I'll give you a clue. Sincere *Martini* might be more to the point... or *Liebfraumilch*?'

He was silently killing himself.

'Lilith Hugg.'

Suddenly all you could hear from the back room was the hissing of gas jets.

'Technically excellent, of course,' said Robin, oblivious

to the hush that had broken out, 'but a bit lacking in ... I've been sending him to life classes at the tech to draw naked ladies, perhaps that will help.'

I stared until my eyeballs pricked, trying vainly to process this new information; to picture square-jawed, Martens-wearing, face-flattening Boy huddled over a drawing board for the hours it must have taken to produce this careful image. 'You mean Boy—' I lowered my voice '—Boy *Hugg* did this?' For some reason, the information depressed me.

'Surprised? It's what makes my job worthwhile, Harry, little surprises—' becoming suddenly earnest '—it's what makes *life* worthwhile. Beauty flowering where you least expect it.'

Some change in the quality of the air then caused me to look up and I saw the Artist standing in the doorway to the back room, fixing me with the sort of look you see in slaughterhouses as the workers square up to the livestock, bolt guns in hand. At the sight of that look something frozen in the rear of my brain flash-thawed and began to drip melt water down the back of my spine. In bed that night, as I lay staring up at the ceiling rose and listening to Amy cough, I could feel it still, playing over the surface of my face like a malevolent ray.

II

I took to varying my route home from school. On successive evenings the journey back to Cato Road took me via the beach, the far side of the park and the council estate which dipped briefly but populously into the Wentworth catchment area. It was here on Friday night, following a cut along the backs of houses while street-lights turned from red to amber to Lucozade yellow, that I rounded the corner by a weeping willow and almost ran straight into the very person I'd been trying to avoid.

He was toe to toe in heated conversation with Anne Singleton, which puzzled me until I remembered that Colin Garganey, Anne's current boyfriend, was Boy's best mate. I ducked hurriedly back behind the corner of a fence. Their voices came to me through the still, cold air, Boy doing most of the talking. He seemed angry. As I listened, it soon became clear why. '... I mean, coming up to me in the high street like that, going on about my mother: I tell you, I'm going to kill the little fucker—'

'He probably didn't mean anything by it, Boy. Harry just overhears bits and pieces and puts them together all wrong. Libby doesn't tell him everything.'

'I thought you said they were close?'

'They are close. Maybe she just thinks it's better to keep him in the dark. Maybe she's scared he wouldn't love her any more if he knew what she gets up to.'

'Weird fucking family.'

'In some ways.'

'Let's stop talking about them.'

A false little giggle came into Anne's voice. 'Why? What would you rather talk about instead?'

Peering around the corner of the fence I watched Boy lead her under the willow. The two figures moved through a tracery of branches to the trunk, where Boy stopped and leant towards her, his face half in darkness, the lighted portion scribbled over by shadows of leafless twigs. Whispers steamed in the Lucozade-coloured street lighting; then there was a sudden intake of breath from Anne and I saw her place an admonitory hand on his arm. 'What about Colin?' she said.

'What *about* him?'

'I thought you and he were best mates.'

Boy said something inaudible which made her laugh uneasily. When he moved forward again, she tilted her head back compliantly. I caught her murmur as their lips met, 'I've always fancied you.'

Was this really Anne, who not so long ago had trapped me in her bedroom and forced me to play Yahtzee with her for three straight hours – Anne the Yahtzee Nazi?

Nose breathing against Boy's cheek, groping the tented front of his Sta-prest, not only letting him feel under her bra but even helping him with the catch...I was close enough from where I stood to see the blouse tucked into the top of her tights when he pulled up her skirt; to read the M & S label on her regulation navy blues...then I had to look away. Dropping my smarting eyes I saw something moving among the frost-dried leaf detritus around my feet: a foraging snail, horns blindly straining.

Careful not to crunch any dry leaves, I tiptoed away.

Libby was waiting for me back at the house, tensely flicking the pages of a magazine.

'What's that smell?' I asked.

She gestured at some jam tarts cooling in front of her on the kitchen table. 'Baking. I've started baking things, like a proper mother, like Mrs Miniver.'

'Who's Mrs Miniver?'

'Never mind – look, before you slouch off to your room, I'm going round to Lilith's tomorrow for coffee.'

'So you'll be wanting me to baby-sit.'

'Anne's doing that. I want you to come along.'

'What?'

She turned around to get another from the pile of *Vogue*s behind her. 'To keep Boy occupied. We girls can chat, you can chuck a ball around or something...I think I'll *scream* if she drags her bloody Avon catalogue out again. Can you imagine it? Ding dong, Big Lil calling...'

'Sometimes you have to tackle things head-on,' she told me later, hugging her knees on the sofa in the sitting room. 'Take the bull by the whatever.'

Obviously, Clem had got to her. I sat hunched in the armchair opposite, trying not to look at her coltish calves, wondering what she was up to.

'I offered a while ago to explain about the Huggs and me, but you didn't seem interested. Maybe I'd better do that now.' She walked over to the corner bay and plucked a piece of Housemartin & Son notepaper off the grand piano, bringing it over to where I was sitting. 'See this?'

'The new letterhead.'

'Any idea how much this stuff costs? Look at it: full colour, gilt embossed. Feel the thickness of the paper.'

'Dad being extravagant again?'

She rolled her eyes. 'There's a pile of it up to the ceiling at the factory; as well as new brochures, signs, the lot. None of it paid for. The bill was due last March – March! There's no money to pay for it, and there won't be next month either. You see, the business is in deep trouble. Orders have been going steadily down over the last few years. That's why we don't go on holiday any more, why you had to change school – luckily Cyril managed to wangle you into a decent state grammar... We're in trouble, basically, and now we've got this whacking great printer's bill we can't pay.'

'Can I guess who the printer is?'

'You're so sharp you could cut yourself. It hasn't been a problem before because Johnson's a friend and he's been prepared to be understanding – but now Lilith is kicking up a stink.'

'Why?'

'She's got it in her head that Johnson has an ulterior motive.'

'Ulterior motive?'

'She thinks I'm sleeping with him...Do you know what bankrupt means, Harry?'

'Of course I do.' I hunched further forward in the armchair.

'We're mortgaged up to the hilt. If she manages to force Johnson into foreclosing the house would go, the car – everything. I've never gone a bundle on this house, as you know, but I don't exactly relish the thought of being chucked out into the street.'

'Is that why Lilith Hugg tried to commit suicide?'

The hard dark lustre of her eyes. 'Who said anything about suicide?'

I stared down at the carpet. 'You were lying, weren't you? That story about the fag butt. You knew the fire wasn't an accident.'

'Okay, so hang me.'

'Has Lilith got any reason to think...what she thinks?'

'Of course not.'

'Well, this might sound naïve, but why don't you just tell her so?'

'That's what I'm going to do tomorrow.'

'And I have to come as Boy's punch-bag – so he can hit me instead of you.'

'Boy's not going to be punching anybody...Look at me, Hal.' She was stood squarely in front of my chair, feet apart on the rug, arms on her hips, bosom thrust righteously forwards. 'I'm your mother. I've got your best interests at heart.'

We eyed each other suspiciously.

III

'Stair-rods,' pronounced Libby next morning. Lodging a tartan cake tin resolutely under one arm, she opened her umbrella and set off down the path. I shambled after her bare-headed between the dripping trees.

It had been an active night. Blood had oozed, squirted and sprayed, clotted gouts of it stiffening hair, spotting flesh. Bone had cracked and teeth crumbled. Wrists had turned to rubber as I rained punches on the huge, scowling shovel of a face which loomed up to menace me. Punches which fell like feathers.

Libby's umbrella was waiting outside the gate. I pulled back when she tried to gather me under it and followed the sound of clicking heels up Cato Road at a resentful distance. But at the lights she pounced, clamping my arm under hers. 'I will not walk five yards ahead of you like some bloody mullah's wife,' she said. 'Anyway, I've got something to tell you, about Anne.' She stepped back smartly as the 17 steamed through a flooded gutter.

Anne had arrived ashen-faced that morning and had talked with Libby up in her room for some quarter of an hour. 'You're not to say anything, but it's Colin. He's broken it off with her. Somebody told him they'd seen her with her hand down some other chap's trousers. An anonymous informant, apparently, calling from a coin-box – I mean, what sort of person *does* a thing like that?'

I looked for signs of the fire as we approached Bearlands. A few new-looking roof tiles, some fresh paint: apart from that, nothing... Though the air was filled with the promise of further disaster. The slap and grunt of volleyball from the fire station next door which greeted our arrival outside the tall wrought-iron gates was the sound of mishaps as yet unimagined, accidents waiting to happen.

Halting at a mock-Georgian porch extension with mullioned panes, Libby's pale hand, ungloved, floated between carriage lamp and horse brass to ring the bell. I shuddered. A moving shape – unidentifiable behind an inner door of bevelled glass – swam towards us from out of the darkness of the house, resolving as it swelled.

Johnson Hugg was the hairiest man I'd ever seen. Thick clumps of the stuff bulked out the cuffs and neck of his Marks & Spencer plaid shirt, sprouting from his cheeks above the stubble line and marching up the bridge of his nose. 'So this is young Harold,' he growled, putting down a bucket of ashes he'd been carrying, extending a hand full of stubby fingers on which grew patches of what looked like cockroach antennae. He crushed my knuckles with careful attention, then we were hustled through into a hall smelling of boiled potatoes.

Libby hadn't been exaggerating about this place: flounces and bows on everything that wasn't Artexed, leprous flock wallpaper and carpet like regurgitated pizza. But despite its garish decoration, its mullion-paned doors, the house felt dark. The light that entered through its bay windows seemed not to penetrate the heart of the building.

'Particularly nasty weather,' mumbled Johnson in Libby's ear as she stooped to rest her umbrella against the door-frame. She giggled, then straightened up smartly at the sight of the figure coming down the stairs. I recognized Boy's mother from his supremely unflattering drawing of her that I had seen in the art room a few days before; but in this case truth was even uglier than fiction. It took an age for Mrs Hugg to reach us and all the while the faded eyes twitched in the heavy face: from Johnson, to Libby, to the leaned umbrella, to the drips it was shedding on the carpet, then back to Johnson.

'I've brought a little something,' Libby said, proffering the cake tin. I guessed that my mother was trying hard not to gawk at Mrs Hugg's velour lounge suit, whose bright magenta made her face, under the shock of white hair, look completely bloodless.

'Too kind,' Lilith wheezed, then made a grab for the umbrella. 'Tupperware's more hygienic though, Elizabeth; those old tins harbour Germans . . . *Germs.*' Laughing a high, nervous laugh she stepped into the porch and held the umbrella over the threshold to shake the silk out, which she did with surprising violence, afterwards dropping it – pank – into a nearby litter bin. She had big hands, I noticed, as big as a man's. In the silence that followed this confusing gesture, scrotum tightening footsteps moved across an upper room. Libby stared blankly at her cake tin, which Lilith showed no signs of accepting.

'And this is Harry,' my mother said, quickly changing tack.

Mrs Hugg jerked her head round to face me.

'Is Boy——?' I began, looking up at the ceiling, my voice buzzing kazoo-like in my ears.

'Boy's been called to an emergency rugby practice.'

'Such a shame,' smiled Libby. 'Hal was looking forward to meeting him properly.'

Lilith rounded on her. 'It's perfectly all right,' she snapped, suddenly furious. 'He'll be back any minute! And Christian's here for him!'

Another, tenser silence.

'I'll leave you girls to it then,' said Johnson. He winked furtively at Libby and loped off through the kitchen towards a louvred extension.

'Excuse me, Mrs Hugg,' I asked. 'Where's your——?'

'Eh? Oh. Downstairs WC is through the kitchen. We're all en suite here...But come in the lounge, Elizabeth. Come in the lounge. You too, Harry, when you've done your business. Christian's here for you somewhere. *Chriss-ie!* Now, Libby, a drink? I mean a hot drink, of course. Tea or Nescafé...?'

In the downstairs bathroom I locked the door and leant against it, chest thumping. I could have wept, out of sheer self-pity. Wept into the pink water of the toilet.

More or less everything in there was pink. It was like being inside somebody's mouth. The carpet was shockingly pink – presumably to match the salmon pink bathroom suite with its brass dolphin taps, as well as the pink loo-seat cover. Pink, too, though paler with repeated washing, was a crescent of rug around the foot of the pedestal which emanated ammonia and a fishy undernote of old piss. *We aim to please*, read a pokerwork sign, *will you aim too, please?*

When I went through to the living room Boy's younger brother was slouching by the patio doors, ostensibly watching the rain sputting up from the crazy paving, but really getting in as many sly glances up Libby's skirt as he could.

'Hi,' I said.

Chrissie took after Lilith. From her, you could see, he got his porridgy skin, his run-to-fat-but-nowhere-else-if-I-can-help-it muscle tone. He had the same bile-coloured eyes, which didn't even flicker recognition as he walked past me and out of the room.

'Run along, dear,' said Lilith, motioning me after him.

Libby, sitting in the window seat with a fag going and a catalogue open beside her, attempted a brave smile.

There was a story that Chrissie Hugg once kept a couple of mice in his desk named Hymie and Manny. When somebody asked him what he was feeding them on he said he wasn't. That was the point. One lunch time he invited a few friends to a 'shower party' in the back room of Art One and gassed them to death.

I caught up with him on the stairs, where he had paused to fart, a long sound like tearing linen. Dropping back a step or two I followed him up to a landing at the end of which more stairs led up to the master bedroom (again, no sign of a fire). On the left, a north-facing room had been converted into a studio. We turned right into the large bedroom the two boys shared.

The room smelled of sperm. Throwing himself down on the nearer of the two beds, Chrissie picked up a spud gun and a pock-marked potato and motioned me towards the other. I was examining a Roxy Music poster on which someone had written in spidery pencil – spidery because the woodchip underneath had forced the point to produce extra curves and loops – KILLER, WHAT'S INSIDE OF YOU?, when a pellet stung my earlobe. I looked over. Chrissie was drawing a bead on me down the blue metal barrel. 'Good customer, your mother,' he said: 'Tarts use a lot of make-up.'

'She thinks of it as charitable giving.'

'Boy beat a policeman up last year, did you know that?'

'Did he?'

'They put in a psychological report. Lack of Affect: know what that means?'

I didn't, but nodded all the same. 'Don't the police pass things like that on to the school?'

'Fuck off. Dad's in the same lodge as the chief copper.'

He cocked his ear as the voices from downstairs started to rise. A look spread over his face for which smirk would be too kindly a word. 'Nice tits. What is she: thirty-six, thirty-seven?'

'Thirty-two.'

'Cup size?'

'I beg your pardon.'

'Cup size?'

'Fuck off.'

'I'd have a fucking permanent bone-on being around

her all the time.' Chrissie fished a crumpled soft-pack of Marlboro from under his mattress and lit up. 'Do you think about her when you're wanking?'

'Fuck off.'

'Wanking your little winky?'

'Fuck off.'

Things were hotting up downstairs by the sound of it, a note of anger entering the muffled voices coming up through the floor. 'Malcolm said that your mother was trying to top herself when she started the fire. Why would she do a thing like that?'

Chrissie shrugged. 'Ask your mother. It was her fucking fault.'

'Was it?'

'Because of what happened at the party.'

'What party?'

A sudden change came over his puddingy features, belligerence morphing into amused incredulity. 'You're telling me you don't know? There was a party here on the night of the fire and your mum was at it. Johnson had her and her friends back here after the pub. They left before the fire brigade showed up, naturally, but they were all here. Your mother, that cunt Butler . . .' He reeled off a list of the inner circle.

'So what happened?'

'Jesus! What colour is the sky on your planet, Mouthmartin?' He teased the ash from his cigarette into a jamjar lid that he was using for an ashtray. Downstairs an argument had definitely broken out, occasional groups of words peaking into intelligibility, 'Blah blah blah blah *Dare* you say blah blah blah blah *Heard* such a load of . . .'

'So what happened?'

'Your mother did a strip, didn't she?' Chrissie chuckled with a lubricious croak. 'Right down to the buff. Lilith had gone to bed early but she got woken up by this banging noise in the plumbing. Came downstairs and saw it all.'

'I don't believe you.'

'Come on, she likes to show it, doesn't she? You can't pretend you haven't noticed.'

'I don't know what you're talking about.'

'The way she dresses – the *life modelling*.'

I snorted my contempt. 'She doesn't *do* life modelling.'

'Jesus!' He began to laugh uncontrollably. 'Jesus Christ! Are you sure you're related to this woman? You don't seem to know a fucking thing about her... Go on, you sorry cunt. Take a look under that bed.'

An unearthed charge crackled along my skin then penetrated inwards, making my bones ache with a heavy, pressed-in heat. Kneeling, I lifted the valance. The space behind it was rammed with sketchpads, the largest of which Chrissie motioned me to pull out and open. Light bled at the corners of my vision, darkening the image on the page.

Somewhere a Yale key meshed with the tumblers of a lock.

'That's your mum, isn't it?' said Chrissie.

'My mother.'

'Jesus wept – you're like a fart in a trance... Your mum. Calling you.'

I listened. Libby's voice seemed to come from a long way off. The sketchpad was plucked from my hands and without quite knowing how I'd got there I found myself at the top of the stairs, looking down at two foreshortened figures against the pizza-vomit carpet. Libby and Boy.

'Time we went, Hal,' called Libby, tremulously.

Somewhere a woman was screaming.

IV

Somewhere a woman was screaming, furniture was being overturned, glass smashed (later I worked out that the noise came from the conservatory at the end of the louvred extension, where Lilith had gone to shy pot plants at her husband). Meanwhile in the hall, Boy, who'd just arrived back from his rugby practice, was staring at my mother with a silent, furious intensity.

She couldn't get out of there fast enough. 'Oh God,' she groaned as we hurried down the drive, 'Oh *God!*'

We came to a halt at the first set of lights. 'You wouldn't believe what I've just been through.' Automatically I took the umbrella so that she could fish a minuscule hand-kerchief from the sleeve of her raincoat. 'Next time I have a great idea like that just shoot me...Oh God!'

The rain had stopped now and the sun was out. Cars threw up brilliant plumes of spray.

'And I've got the Parks's coming round in half an hour to take me to lunch – *and* Martin's due back this afternoon... Hal, what am I going to do?'

She looked at me with reddened eyes that pleaded for pity; that didn't want questions or accusations but the sort of uncritical love I used to bombard her with, in the days before that fateful encounter in the high street. However, the shock of those pages had been too numbing; I couldn't feel anything for her except astonishment at the unfamiliar thing she'd suddenly become. We stared at each other until she looked away, unnerved.

The lights changed and we crossed, walking the rest of the way home in silence.

Anne Singleton answered the door, darting an insultingly brief glance in my direction before fastening on my mother. 'What is it, Libby?'

'Come upstairs.'

They disappeared together into the upper reaches of the stairwell and I slumped onto the ottoman, focusing somewhere beyond the faded green baize of the servants' door. Colour was leaching from the world.

When everybody had gone, leaving me alone in the house with the sleeping Amy, I took a bath to calm my nerves. I didn't know whether to believe Chrissie or not, but there was no arguing with what I'd seen. Sheet after sheet of boss-eyed glaring breasts, spread legs; Boy's forensic pencil hatching unguessable geometries: the trained sit of the vertebrae, the notch of a hip, the intricate mystery of the vulva. They zinged on my retinas, these images, reanimating long-forgotten memories of Libby fresh out of the shower, wrapped in a tiny guest towel knotted over her breasts and singing along to the radio. Baby love. Stop, Mummy. Baby love. Stop dancing, Mummy. Miss kissin' ya. *Stop, it makes my willy hurt.*

The towel coming open.

And other memories, hardly memories at all: burnings and shivers, torpors and sudden shocks.

I padded back towards my room, head reeling. At that moment, a stray draught – a peppery zephyr – came at me along the landing, stopping me in my tracks, and I noticed that Libby's bedroom door hung ajar.

She'd changed in a hurry for her lunch with the Parks's. Clothes were thrown everywhere, make-up in disarray. I moved as if on rails towards her wardrobe, savouring its perfumed breath, sliding a hand inside. Taffeta and slub slipped squeaky dry between my finger pads. Light as a whisper, a lissom slip spilled from its plastic wishbone and snagged my prick, which I noticed with eerie detachment was as stiff as a chairleg.

A strange vacancy came over me then, rummaging through her knicker drawer, fingering umbral lace and floreate cotton, rolled up balls of stocking and the thrilling web of a suspender belt. Normally the thought alone would have rendered me quadriplegic with shame, but I felt calm. Calm? Mine was the tranced serenity of bankrupts, defrocked priests, rumbled bigamists, serial killers once the extra friends under the floorboards have come up to be counted. Cosmic abandon, astral relief. Spreading puckered black pants and bras against the white of her coverlet – loosening the knot of blood, letting the milt gush – I felt calm.

Cleaned up and back in my own room though, not so calm.

'All right, Amy?'

The ill child looked fuddled and pillow-streaked, waking from a deep sleep.

'Fancy a story?' Already my fingers were skipping along the bookshelf's knackered spines. These books, with their grave-marked pages, their smell of must; the infant scrawl defacing their end papers – my naim is harry i am sicks – seemed to offer talismanic reassurance.

But Amy had other things on her mind. 'I'm frightened of Willie,' she whimpered.

It took a heart-stopping second or two, in my deranged state, for me to realize that she was talking about the bear in the park zoo.

'Will you look under the bed?'

'Was this a dream, Amy?'

'He escaped from the zoo. I thought he was nice but he's not.'

'Amy, let me read you a story.'

'He was under my bed, humping and bumping me, and he just wouldn't stop.'

'Dreams are dreams, Amy, real is real. Look, what about this one. *The Tinder Box*?'

'I want you to go and check he's still in his cage.'

'Don't be silly—'

'Plee-*ease*! I'm scared.'

'*Mumfy? River of Adventure?*' I threw volume after volume onto her rose-coloured eiderdown but still she wheedled. 'Amy, you know I can't leave you alone in the house.'

Her agitation had sparked another coughing fit. 'You've got to go and make sure he's still there.' – *Cough* – 'NOW!'

'Okay then, but not until Libby gets back.'

I heard a door slam downstairs.

The park was empty. The sun had gone in and the air held a damp, bone-withering cold. Guessing that Willie would be in sulking rather than basking mode, I went straight round to the back of the converted stable block that housed the animals' indoor quarters and was almost knocked flat by its smell of shit and rotting veg. But there was Willie all right, a sad brown hump among the heaps of sawdust that you might have taken for a discarded car coat if it hadn't been for the slow regular movement of his breathing.

As I stared at the slumbering creature, waiting for my eyes to adjust to the gloom, a face appeared reflected in the scratched yellow Plexiglas of the window and I realized that Boy had slipped into the dark space beside me.

V

'So what did you want to talk to me about?' He lit a cigarette and let the smell of it seep into the rank air, waiting.

'First of all,' I said, falteringly, 'that thing in the high street. To apologize. I didn't know your mother had tried to commit suicide, I was just parroting what I'd overheard from Libby.'

'Yeah, and?'

'Also I wanted to ask you what the big thing was between you and my mother.'

The coin box at the corner of the road, the same one I'd used to inform on him and Anne, was where I'd called him from. On the phone he'd been tight-lipped, his tone neutral. I watched anxiously now as his expression changed, his nostrils twitching in disgust, his mouth turning down at the corners. 'It fucking honks in here,' he said.

We took a walk by the football field. He screwed his eyes up at the far end of the field where men in coloured shirts were running and shouting, shouting and running. 'Man on, Bal' – 'To me, Mal.' 'Libby. What's that short for?'

'Dunno. I've always just called her Libby.'

'You mean you don't know your own mother's name?'

'Is it important?'

'She used a different one at the tech.'

'At the tech?'

'For life modelling.'

'Oh.'

'Linane. Linane Dunlin.' Dunlin was Libby's maiden name.

He took me to the park café and bought me a cup of tea, most of which I managed to slop in the saucer.

'Cig?'

'No thanks.'

I watched him sketch the outline of a naked woman in the steamed-up window with a finger. It gave me a queasy feeling. 'Before that day in the high street I had absolutely fuck all idea.'

'Was that why you looked so surprised when you saw her with me?'

'Right, it was seeing her with you . . . I mean, you've got to admit – she doesn't exactly look like someone's mother.'

'Did you talk to her at all? At life classes?'

'Oh yeah, we talked.'

I waited, but this was as specific as he wanted to get. 'So why did you call her a *lying slag*?'

'It was her fault my mother almost topped herself; how do you expect me to react?' I looked at the torso he'd sketched in the condensation-frosted window. Its lines had begun to drip and run.

'Because of what happened at the party. What *did* happen at the party?'

'I need to talk to her,' he said, chucking his cigarette butt into his tea, which he hadn't touched.

'Why not just ring her up?'

'Because she puts the phone down, Brainiac fucking Five.'

'What do you want to talk to her *about*?'

He glared at the melamine tabletop. 'You ought to be able to sort something out.'

'I still don't understand—'

An irritated flickering of the eyelids. Raising his head he gave me a look that threatened to weld my rods to my cones. 'She may be the local shagbag, she may have fucked me about like nobody's business, but I can't help it if I fucking love her, can I? I fucking love the bitch!'

Love her? Black was white. Up was down.

'She came on friendly enough at the tech, but soon as she finds out I'm one of the nouveau fucking Huggs ... I'm not being frozen out like that. I want to talk to her, alone – hear me? And you're going to help.' He stood up abruptly. 'You'd better help or else you're going to end up drinking your tea out of a fucking plastic tube ...' With a backhanded swipe he sent his ignored cup and saucer rattling across the tabletop towards mine. They collided, falling into my lap and then noisily smashing on the floor.

Counter staff stared outraged at the broad back retreating towards the door. I sat rooted to the spot, cold tea soaking through to my thighs.

★

I'd hoped to avoid Libby back at the house, but she nabbed me in the kitchen, jabbering in my ear about not mentioning the Hugg business in front of Martin, whose mustard Volvo I'd noticed blocking the drive.

'And by the way, Hal, have you been in my room?'

'No.'

'Sure?' She struggled vainly to catch my eye.

'What would I be doing in your poxy room?'

'Go on then,' she said eventually. 'Go and see if you can make contact.'

As I pushed through the baize-covered swing door into the gloomy hall, slinking sullenly towards the sound of the television, stained-glass fruit glowed plum and viridian in the panels flanking the front door. An architect had built this house. Then hanged himself, not long after he'd finished it, from the quince tree in the orchard. *We've got a visitor*, she'd said. I looked hard at the attenuated silhouette lit cyan by the light of the TV screen. He was watching the news, the coat of a three-piece suit draped over the back of his armchair. Oxfords sat unlaced on the Axminster.

'Dad?'

He turned and regarded me, not fondly but without any particular hostility, in the same way that you might stare at lines on the palm of your hand, wondering how bad the news there might be.

Sour

I

A warm wind moved across the plot stirring uncut grass, winding drying sheets around the prop of the clothes-line and throwing a blizzard of dandelion spores about the orchard. Cloud that had loured over us since Martin's return from Germany blew away and I came down to find the kitchen full of chilly sunlight. The not-particularly-nice-old-thing was in Libby's usual place at the range, glaring hatred at a gloopily bubbling saucepan.

'Everything okay, Mrs Armitage?'

'How could it not be with so much Good News in God's Kingdom?'

Clearly care of the sick (i.e. Amy) on top of normal duties wasn't part of the Good News.

Grabbing a slice of cold toast from the rack and drifting through to the morning room, I spotted Martin shindeep in the grass outside.

My father had spent Christmas in Germany as the house guest of Franz Lammergeier, a business contact of his whom I had met briefly on an ill-fated trip there a couple of years earlier. Evidently, buttering up Franz was more important than spending the holiday with us. From there he'd gone on to meetings in Geneva, trying to raise capital for some joint venture that he and Franz were planning (according to Libby). In all, he'd been out of the country for over two months. Not an unusual occurrence.

Then, on his return to England, Martin's apparent attitude to the house at the bottom of Cato Road had undergone a strange transformation. After all these years my father seemed to have decided that home was where the heart is. He'd taken to hanging around the place non-stop in the two months or so since his return, driving us ga-ga with his brown studies, mealtime conversation so doggedly inconsequential that it forced you to weigh every morsel for coded significance and a generally maddening, adamantine evasiveness. No hint was given about why he was spending so much time with us. A direct question, as I knew from long experience, would have elicited only an embarrassed silence and would have been treated as an unfortunate lapse of manners to be tactfully ignored. Knowledge of his plans and movements wasn't something you had a right to just because you happened to be related to him. For her part, Libby seemed reluctant to be drawn on the subject, and my problems with regard to her — those wanton stiffies — made me unwilling to press the matter.

Right now, Martin was staring at a sky across whose blankly cheerful expanse some departing jet had strewn a contrail like a stripper's feather boa. To judge from the wood saw dangling limply at his side something was scheduled to be sawn up, presumably one of our diseased elms – though you wouldn't want to ask precisely what, for fear of that wounded, distant look coming over him. I waited, balanced on the metal frame of the French windows, while he gradually became aware of my existence. It started with a series of almost imperceptible tensings – the rounded back straightening, the hand that held the saw stiffening as if with remembered purpose – followed by a sidling round of one hazel eye to catch me in peripheral vision. 'Not at school today then.' He raised a senatorial arm.

'Day off.'

'For what?'

'Founder's day... Any idea where Libby might be?'

He ignored the question, which I suspected he couldn't answer. 'Somebody telephoned for you, did Mrs Armitage say? Johnson Hugg's eldest; wouldn't leave a message, said you'd know what it was all about.'

I opened my mouth to speak, but already he was sliding away, moving nervously, apprehensively even, through his grove of trees.

We had never bonded, my father and I. Looking back I now wonder if the trip to Germany that we had taken together – his idea – had perhaps been intended as a repairing of this breach. In which case it had been a miserable failure.

I watched him disappear around the side of the house, simultaneously vanishing from conscious thought.

Hardly a morning went by now without Boy slamming

me up against some wall or other to demand a progress report. Our relationship had come on by leaps and bounds. During less pressured sessions, when he would seek me out at the back of the hall in a study period, or in some discreet corner of the library, I would share with him knowledge of my mother's tastes and foibles accumulated over a decade and a half.

There seemed no end to his appetite for Libby-related trivia. He listened rapt to my description of her packaging fetish – how she loved to shred tissue paper, slough the Cellophane from a new shirt, peel blue Fyffes stickers off bananas and attach them to my eyelids while I slept. Likewise her obsession with shoes. Libby's favourite type of building (I told him) was a shoeshop, her favourite smell in the whole world new leather. Couldn't you just see her in Freeman, Hardy and Willis snuffing its oaky, tannic nose, slapping her thigh principal boy-style and booming 'BLESS your beautiful hide!'? Only, when it came to questions of a more factual, biographical nature, I showed a disturbing tendency to dry up.

We were constantly recycling the Housemartin myth-trove at home; Ernst coming to England penniless, building up a business in industrial ceramics and changing his name from Mauer-Schwalbe at a time when sausage dogs were being drop-kicked through shop windows... but the Dunlins? Here, matrilineal recounting fell bafflingly silent.

And what of my primary task, the task for whose accomplishment Boy had chosen today as the deadline – getting Libby to meet Boy alone? She was coming round, I'd told him. Bit by bit she was beginning to see things our way. Bollocks she was. What with Martin around so much, what with the candour-killing gas he seemed to emit, I hadn't even managed to broach the subject. Hence Founder's day, a fiction designed to put off if for only a little longer the moment when Boy would have to be told the unpleasant truth. Hence my desperate need to locate Libby.

I shuddered despite the mildness of the air. Putting a record on the stereogram, I stepped barefoot into rippling grass. At the same moment as the needle started crackling in the run-in groove came the hesitant creak of a hand-brake from the drive and next thing Libby was pushing her way through the sheets on the washing line. Windborne, lifted tips of hair framed a kilowatt smile.

Here she comes.

'Hal, I've got the most incredible news!'

In an instant her arms were wrapped around my neck and she was pressing her face against mine. 'Oh, Hal,' she said. 'My Harry! Isn't it wonderful – I passed my test!'

'Didn't even know you were retaking it,' I said, shivering for her, braless under the mohair sweater.

'I've wanted to do this so many times in the last few months.' A tearful sniff. Then a second, suspicious sniff. 'When did you last have a bath? You smell like—' she buried her nose in my kitchen scissors crop '—like marrowfat peas.' I was given the maternal once-over: dimmed expression, spotty skin. 'You don't smile enough ... Look at this glorious day!' Her kohl-rimmed eyes widened with girlish enthusiasm. 'Music! Sunshine—' she jingled her car keys '—full driving licence! ... What's the record?'

'Velvet Underground with Nico. "Femme Fatale".'

She's gong to break your hut in two.

'Are we friends again? Come here.'

We certainly weren't anything like friends. Over the weeks and months since that afternoon in the park, something of Boy's strangely contradictory attitude towards Libby had bled into mine. He'd shown me a way to hate her. In fact at that moment I hated her so badly that I was beginning to think about retreating to the bathroom, when suddenly she said, 'Oh, Hal, I'm so happy – let's go for a drive into town!'

An intense warmth, a ray of heavenly manumission seemed to play over my scalp. Before that moment I'd despaired of a chance to talk to her alone. Away from the house, though, away from Martin, who knows . . . ? Just as suddenly, hopes seemed to fade as Libby's attention was drawn to a barking saw in the garden. 'Don't tell him,' I blurted. 'I mean, not just yet . . . You know what a wet blanket he can be.'

'You're right; he'd only find some way of bringing me down and I don't want to be brought down just yet . . . Oh, come on, let's do it! Get something on your feet. Try and do something to make yourself look human while I square things Mrs Armitage-wise.'

As I ran water in the basin in my room the two women's voices came up from the kitchen. To judge by the tone of Mrs Armitage's she wasn't taking this latest Good News lying down. But presently, things having been squared, Libby appeared thumbs-up in the doorway wearing a headscarf and her biggest, blackest sunglasses. See the way she woks, hear the way she tocks.

II

'Christ, Mother!'

A horn blew. The tyres of the Volvo shushed horrify-ingly as it slewed to a stop. 'Where'd you get your licence, love?' called a taxi driver with a face like smeared newsprint, rapidly cranking down his window. 'In a facking Christmas cracker?'

'Pig!' sang Libby. Throwing her sunglasses down on the dashboard, she refired the ignition.

'He's got a point,' I said.

'Hal!' she cried, horrified at my disloyalty. 'It's because I'm a woman.'

'Nothing to do with you coming at him the wrong way up a one-way street.'

'*I* didn't see any signs.' She slammed the car into a bumper-nudging three-point turn and we set off again.

'Mind that pram!'

'I knew it was there. Hal, don't be so jumpy; what's got into you today?'

Her slashed satin skirt parted over one thigh as she pumped the pedals. This was going to be far more difficult than I'd envisaged. 'Libby,' I said, looking determinedly in the other direction. 'Can I ask you a question?'

'Uh-huh?' She frowned at the rear end of the car in front.

'Why didn't you tell me about the life modelling?'

'What life modelling, dear?'

'You know what I'm talking about...Look, perhaps we should just drop the subject if it's going to make you veer all over the road like this.'

'I wasn't veering. I'm totally capable of driving and talking at the same time, thank you.'

'You're supposed to stop at zebra crossings.'

'There wasn't anyone *on* it!'

'Look, the life modelling. It's no good denying it; Boy told me.'

She was silent for a moment or two. Then she took a bosom-inflating breath. 'Bloody Boy...you haven't told Martin, have you? I'll pull your arms and legs off if you've told your father.'

'Sure you wouldn't rather wait until we get to the high street?'

'I'm perfectly fine...Oh God...I did it for the money, Hal. Just to have some money of my own. I mean, where would we be if—'

'You get better money stacking shelves in Tesco.'

'Can you see me in one of those vile gingham housecoats?'

'At least you'd have something on.'

'Is the idea of me naked so repellent?'

She turned to look at me. I tried to swallow but my mouth was too dry. 'Shouldn't you keep your eyes on the—'

'Nonsense, it's like typing; you do it by feel.'

'Well, it's obviously not repellent to Boy, is it?' I said, as she returned her gaze to the road. 'I know all about his crush on you. Another little thing you never got around to telling me.'

Carefully painted lips parted, then clamped shut. A silence fell, in which I imagined I could hear both our hearts thumping – a silence which she tried to fill by clicking on the radio, only to find that Martin had left one of his cartridges in the machine. The car was filled with a skirl of stereorama strings – Mahler Five – which she angrily clicked off. 'Bloody German death music. Why is there nowhere to park around here?'

'You have to go to the multistorey.'

'I didn't *waggle* anything at him, if that's what you think.'

'Like you used to at me.'

'Shut up, Hal.'

'You don't even realize you're doing it, do you? Like when you got up this morning and put on that skirt. I bet you didn't consciously think: I know, I'll flash my knickers at the examiner—'

'Hal, how *dare* you!'

'I'm sorry. Forget I said it. The point is, I'm supposed to arrange some sort of meeting between you and Boy or else he's going to beat me to a pulp. He keeps telephoning me.'

'You too. Tell me what that sign we just passed means again.'

'Buses and taxis only... Talk to him, Libby, that's all I'm asking. Sometimes you have to meet these things head-on, remember; take the bull by its—'

'Hal, Boy Hugg is another country; they do things differently there. You just don't know what you're asking.'

'I'm asking you to save my neck.'

'I'd have to be mad, I'd have to be stark staring bonkers ... Let me tell you something about this Boy Hugg you seem to be so matey with all of a sudden. I told you Anne had been seen with someone other than Colin, but you don't know the full story.'

'Yes, I do. I was there. And it was me that made the phone call, after I saw her feeling him up.'

'Hal! How could you do such a thing!'

'Don't you have any conception of fidelity whatsoever? She was cheating on her boyfriend.'

'So you didn't see the rape then.'

'What rape?'

'You can't have done. Listen, the reason Anne was so upset when she came round was that Boy raped her.'

'It didn't look much like rape to me.'

'They started off with heavy petting, but Anne would never have gone beyond that. Boy just doesn't take no for an answer. He forced her. And he didn't even do it the normal way; he did it ... you know.'

'I *don't* know.'

'Up the bottom, for God's sake – do I really have to spell it out?'

'What if Anne's making all this up just to get off the hook with Colin?'

'I don't believe you could think that of her.'

'Chicks. You stick together like shit to a blanket.'

That got her Paddy dander up, the colour rushing to her cheeks. 'It isn't like that, Hal, I've got ample reason to believe her in this case.'

'What reason?'

'I know what Boy's like.'

'How?'

'God, you're never satisfied are you? Never satisfied until you squeeze out the last bloody pip... Because something horribly similar almost happened to me at life class. That's why I gave up going. Boy tried to rape me.'

Drums tumbling ceaselessly in the windows of Planters threw up a fine efflorescence that permeated the long low room. You could sense its narcotic effects on the staff: anxious, bloodshot ectomorphs, nails at the quick, they had that rhythmless urgency to their movements. That numbed alertness. A mocha gerontion scurried over to the quiet corner we had chosen with our coffees, then scurried away again. I watched my mother light a cigarette. She'd seemed pale on the roof of the multi-storey; here, in the filtered yellow light, she glowed falsely healthful.

'Right from the start I noticed him giving me odd looks. Not that I knew who he was then.'

'When did you find out?'

'Not until that awful thing in the high street... Oh, why couldn't you just have kept your mouth shut?'

'Did you talk to him at the life class?'

'A bit. In the breaks.'

'What about?'

'About his work. About the weather. I don't know, Hal, nothing significant... nothing that seemed significant to

85

me, anyway. Then one day he followed me back to the room where I got changed, and... They gave me this little cubicle, hardly more than a broom cupboard, to change in. He followed me back there after the session and barged his way in. God, it was awful. Luckily Barry, the chap who runs the classes heard me screaming, otherwise God *knows* what would have happened.'

'Had you done anything to provoke him; led him on in any way?'

A lungful of smoke issued in my direction. 'It's an insult that you have to ask that question.'

'You can't blame me for asking it.'

'I used to talk to him during the breaks, but only ever about the work... All the models did it: you put on a robe and walked round looking at what they'd drawn. Boy's were easily the best, but I never gave him the slightest indication—'

'And you had absolutely no idea who he was?'

She shook her head, sipping from the cup. 'Not until that moment in the high street.'

'Why didn't you tell me about it then? I mean – afterwards.'

'Because I was too embarrassed.' She looked away at the wall sconces, whose intricately cut metal silhouetted scenes of happy darkies growing and harvesting from the Orient to the Andes. 'I'm embarrassed talking about it now.' She turned a level gaze on my face. A grown-up look. 'Hal, you do understand that there have to be... limits, between a mother and son?'

'I don't remember limits in the old days.'

'Well. More's the pity.' She looked at her watch. 'Drink your coffee, Hal, we can't be out too long.'

'No, wait. There's something else I've got to ask you about.'

'It'll keep.'

'Bearlands, the night of the fire. There was a party and you were at it: Chrissie told me. Lilith came downstairs and...'

She began to fiddle nervously with her handbag. 'Just a silly party that got out of—'

'Chrissie said you did a – you took off your... Libby, what happened that night?'

'Come on, Hal, hurry up. I've had about as much of this as I can take.' Suddenly she was gathering up her cigarettes and lighter and shoving them into her bag. 'Finish your coffee. Martin will be wondering where we are. Mrs Armitage—'

'Libby, this is insane. You can't just not tell me *anything*.'

She raised her arm, signalling for the bill. 'This was going to be such a good day and you ruined it. Just like you ruined Christmas...'

'I overheard Anne telling Boy that you keep things from me because you're scared I won't love you any more, but that's stupid. I won't stop loving you just because you've done a strip in front of a load of men... Okay, it's a bit of a shock, but it doesn't mean—'

'You don't realize the damage you do, Hal. Didn't I try to warn you about the situation we're in?'

'Oh yes, that little speech about all the money we owe Johnson Hugg... I mean, what has owing Johnson loads of dosh got to do with—'

It was like running slap into a wet sandbag.

'Oh, no.'

'Shut *up*, Hal. She's coming over.' I watched my

mother's fingers trembling as they fumbled in her purse, laid coins on the crocheted place mat.

'It wasn't just a striptease, was it?'

Out in the street I struggled to keep up with her. '...Was it, Libby; it wasn't just a bloody striptease, was it?'

To the wind whipping round the corner of Dixons she turned a face of determined intransigence, lips set, eyes blazing.

III

The wind had got up. On the roof of the multistorey I watched it fling my mother's skirt out sideways from her legs like a black flag as she stalked across the tarmac towards the Volvo parked in the corner. She'd insisted on coming up here for a roof view, spiralling erratically through floor after floor of free space. Trailing some ten paces behind and off to the right, I dawdled close by the row of breeze blocks that edged the roof, sick with vertigo as I looked down at shopgirls daydreaming on the escalators of the precinct, Kawasakis threading the underpass; the town, with all its carparks and showrooms, garages and breakers' yards, flyovers, driving schools, carwashes carrying on a formic, circulatory life.

'HAL, HURRY UP!'

'Look at me, Ma,' I cried, hopping onto the breeze-block parapet. 'Top of the world.'

She turned.

A gust of wind buffeted my body and I braced myself, using knees and arms to find balance. The sudden rush of adrenaline seemed to clear my brain: a near neighbour of the calm that had visited me up in Libby's bedroom.

'Hal, come down from there.' As she hurried towards me, skirt flying up from scything thighs, I noticed with a start that I had been wrong about Libby's subconscious thought processes that morning – she hadn't actually put any knickers *on*.

Hands fighting down the skirt, she came to a halt some six or so yards short of the wall. 'Hal, don't do anything stupid.'

Behind her, sun flooded the horizon, fuzzying up the line of chimneys on the Isle of Grain, where the first North Sea oil had come ashore the previous June, the windfall that, according to Clem, was going to guarantee my future for the next ten years. At that moment, I found it hard to see beyond the next ten seconds. The Huggs were taking over. To have nothing to look forward to but further humiliations, to be *under* them forever...

Taking a deep breath I turned into the wind, pivoting slowly on my feet and keeping my eyeline doggedly level. I looked inland, beyond the canyon formed by the civic centre and the tech building, towards Rochford. One of those pregnant-looking car carriers was taking off from the airport. An ungainly miracle. Watching it lift off from the ground gave me an odd sensation of weightlessness, together with the updraught from the wind hitting the side of the building (its sheer edge millimetres from my leading toe) which made me feel as if I too might, equally miraculously, lift off at any moment.

'Hal, please...'

Mother a tart, Father a dalek. And what hope for me, the oldest joke in creation? When he found what he had done, he pulled his eyes out one by one. Before that moment, I'd never troubled to tot it all up – my tardy weaning, the wayward stiffies, the fierce jealousies, wild wet dreams, the resentment of the father – I'd never run my eye down that column of writhing figures to see the sum at the bottom.

Now I did.

After I'd glanced at it once, things around me ceased to register with quite the same intensity. I was only vaguely conscious of the commotion down below – of the shouting, pointing crowd that had gathered – of Libby at my back, finally losing her rag and starting to scream into the keening wind, 'HARRY, COME DOWN, HARRY!' It all receded in the rush of air past my ears and the heightened physical sense I suddenly had of the building's wand-like flexibility. I was becoming its extension. Thought, feeling, froze hard. My head spun with the rotation of the earth: rolling, rushing through space. The idea of falling no longer held any fear, because weren't we all falling, constantly falling? *What did one more tumble—*

Suddenly arms locked around my neck, and Libby was clawing me back over the parapet. 'You *stupid* bastard.' Forcing me to the deck with battering fists. 'You stupid, stupid, little—' Then we were wrestling in the dirt blown into the corner of the wall. Dust, sand and cigarette butts, sweet papers, fish-and-chip wrappers sallow with saveloy grease and she was hitting me, hugging me, smearing my face with her lipstick, wetting me with her tears, cradling my trembling form with arms and laddered thighs.

★

91

Tears coursed freely down her face as she piloted the Volvo inexpertly down the Cliffs road. 'It was all for your sake – all I wanted was for you to have a future... Oh, you don't understand. I suppose I could have told you more; it's just that the world is a horrible place, and maybe I didn't want you to find that out quite yet. You're still a child, really.'

I looked over at the estuary. A sunlit ship was headed for the open sea, far off. But the tide was out; between the water and the land was a mile or more of greyish-brown, scarred and pitted mud, a moron horizontal broken only by the occasional stick-like figure digging for ragworms.

She drove in silence for a while.

'Don't you wish we could roll this day back and start again?' she said at last. 'It began so well: sunshine in the orchard, nice music. I've got that song on the brain now – what was it? Write it down for me so I can buy it for the car.'

'I don't think you can get it on eight-track. No one is releasing on eight-track any more. To tell the truth, eight-track has had it.'

'Well, your father's still buying cartridges – only he can't get the sort of stuff he likes; you know, that German death music.'

Obviously something tugged in me towards the death music – perhaps I was made of the less buoyant, Martin-like stuff. 'Libby. I'm sorry about what happened back there.'

She patted my knee reassuringly, missing a gear change in the process.

Martin was waiting outside the house when we drew up,

looking agitated. He'd changed into a grey business suit and his briefcase was parked beside him on the kerb.

'Passed my test,' Libby called to him, lowering her window. 'Is something wrong?'

'You've left the choke out,' he said, reaching in and pushing the knob back into the dashboard. 'And the tank's nearly empty... Look, I've got to go to Manchester.'

'Why, what's happened?'

The line of his lipless mouth compressed. 'And by the way, Amy's coughed up more blood. Sort of a . . . clot, this time.'

Libby yanked the handbrake and threw the door open in one movement.

'No need to panic; I rang Summerbee. He said just to watch her overnight. He's coming round to do a blood test in the morning.'

She swung her legs around and sat staring up at my father while the breath gathered in her chest. Then, swiping the keys out of the ignition, she sprang out of the car and barged past him through the gate.

'Libby. . .' He grabbed his briefcase from the kerb and trotted after her. 'Give me the keys, darling, I need the car.'

'Get one on the firm,' she flung at him, striding purpose-fully up the drive and round towards the back door.

'You know the firm can't afford—'

'I'm taking her to hospital in it.'

'But Manchester!'

'Get a train. A plane.'

She pulled open the back door and we followed her into the kitchen. 'Hal can call a taxi for you. Oh, I'm sorry: Martin meet Harry; Harry, Martin.'

'Libby—'

She rounded on us in the hall, gesturing me to the telephone: 'Call ten-two-ten. Tell them it's on account.'

'The account's been cancelled,' said Martin flatly. I could see he was puzzled by her dishevelled appearance, her laddered stockings.

'Pay cash, then, like normal people.' With a defiant glare she evaginated her purse onto the parquet floor, then turned towards the stairs.

'Look, Libby,' he called after her, 'I'm sure things are really not that serious; if Summerbee says—'

'That reminds me... *Harry*?' she called, disappearing into the upper reaches of the stairwell, 'ring Doctor Summerbee after I've gone and give him a message from me.'

'What d'you want me to tell him?'

Her voice came down from the attic, the words muffled but still recognizable, 'Tell him he's a wanker.'

I was left stranded in the hall with Martin, who seemed too rigid with embarrassment to speak. They had never argued in front of me. They had never argued. As far as I knew, their entire marriage had been conducted using a recondite sort of code. Reaching for the heavy bakelite receiver, I called the number Libby had given and ordered a cab, then knelt and swept up her contribution to the fare.

'Thank you,' he said bitterly, barely looking at me as he pocketed the coins and notes.

Shortly afterwards Libby called me up to Amy's bedroom. My little sister was burning up, either asleep or unconscious. Libby had packed a small bag to take to the hospital and was changing her stockings.

'God, that man,' she whispered, smoothing hands up her legs. 'Sometimes I wonder why I married him.'

She flicked her skirt down again, then I watched her bending over the bed, cocooning the sleeping child in an eiderdown for the journey.

'Come here and give me a cuddle,' she said, straightening up. Before I could protest she had seized me and was kissing me full on the lips. 'I love you, Hal, you know that, don't you?' She kissed me again. 'Tell me that you know I love you.'

'Leave it out, Mother.'

'But I'm going to miss you—' Her arm looped round my back, pulling me towards her. 'Can't I give my own son a snog? Come here.'

'No – please—'

'It's like the old days, isn't it?' She kissed me again and I abandoned the attempt to push her away, pleasure rippling out from our joined mouths. Then, abruptly, the pressure of her arms relaxed and she stepped back with a little 'Oh' of surprise. My eyes snapped open on her querulous, downward stare.

For a moment I thought she was going to laugh, but she didn't. Instead she walked over to the far corner of the room and started rummaging in her handbag. 'Don't get confused, Hal; I'm your mother, not your girlfriend.'

Despite the three-bar fire, the air in the attic had turned suddenly icy.

'Libby, I've been meaning to tell you—'

'Don't, Hal.' When she turned again, something had switched off behind her eyes. 'Can you carry Amy down to the car please?'

I stared at the floor between us, incredulous. 'What? You think if you ignore it then—?'

'Just don't. Not now.'

'This is important. *I need to talk to you about this*.'

'Keep your voice down, Martin will hear you.'

'How can you ignore it, Libby, after all that's happened?'

'NO – Hal, don't do this to me. Amy needs us she's – look at her – just carry her down.'

Amy was shaking gently, the beginnings of a febrile convulsion. She'd had them before when she was much younger, so we both knew what had to be done, and how urgently – but this seemed more important. 'How do you expect me to go down there like this?' I said, anxious fingers moulding the still-growing lump in the front of my Levis.

She whirled away, horrified. 'Don't *do* that, Hal!' Sobs started to shake the spare frame. Meanwhile Amy was turning grey, her fibrillation intensifying.

'I love you, Mother,' I blurted woefully. 'I mean, I *really* love you—'

'TAXI'S HERE,' yelled Martin from below. 'WELL, ISN'T ANYONE GOING TO COME AND SAY GOODBYE TO ME, FOR GOD'S SAKE?'

Colour was leaching from the world.

'I'm in Hell,' cried Libby, 'I'm really in Hell!'

IV

Night came on and a cloudless sky sucked the warmth from the earth. To the cold, to the baleful stare of constellations and the yelping wind – to my feelings of shame and desolation – I made the atavistic response. In the sitting room I crumbled greasy slabs of firelighter into scrunched-up pages from the *Sunday Times*, added twigs from the orchard and coal from a paper sack, and lit a fire.

Soon tongues of flame were roaring up the chimney at the night sky as, on the television, Bert Ford glowered at isobars menacing the estuary.

The telephone rang. It was Libby. At the hospital they'd examined Amy then put her straight onto a children's ward, attached to a machine that made a bleeping sound. And you knew what it meant when they attached them to a machine that made a bleeping sound . . . ? 'Summerbee deserves to get bloody well struck off over this.'

I agreed, remembering his frigid fingers, his busy tit-man eyes.

'All they say is *tests* . . . You should have seen the size of the needle they used on her, poor darling . . . Trephine, what was it called? I'm going to have to stay overnight. Maybe longer.'

'Okay.'

'How about you, Hal? Are you sure you're going to be all right?'

'Sure. Do I have to go to school in the morning?'

'Of course you do.'

A silence.

'It's all my fault. When I go on about being a bad person, a bad mother, it's not just something I say . . . But don't worry too much, I'm sure it'll just turn out to be a phase or something. We'll get you some help.'

'Help?'

'Just don't worry about it.'

This would be the first night I'd ever spent in the house alone – remarkable really, when you considered Libby's social life. Granted I'd often had to cook my own pan-blackening supper and put myself to bed, but whatever she got up to, wherever she went with her men, some-how she had always managed to make it back before dawn. At some point, whether I was conscious of it or not, there would be the car ventilating in the road outside, the key in the lock; and in the morning her mouth print on my cheek to wash away.

Back at the hearth I resumed my sacerdotal proddings.

It wasn't until an hour or two later, after a Cup-a-soup and a mournful wank, that I noticed the battered A2-sized parcel in the hall addressed to Libby. Leprous and bent after a night in the hands of postal workers, it had little left to hide. I stripped away the rest of its brown paper on the way to the sitting room. Firelight fell across the spread pad and I remembered the sensation of falling I'd experienced when I first turned these pages under Chrissie Hugg's mantic gloat.

Imagine an inhabitant of the Bottle City of Kandor who has managed despite everything to remain unaware of the true condition of his existence, i.e. stashed away on a shelf in Superman's Arctic Fortress. Imagine how he feels on the day when a spiteful fellow Kandorian spills the beans — you live in a bottle, Bud — just to see the look on his face. Paradigm shift they call it: that collapse of mental brackets, that vertiginously sudden reckoning of a larger equation parenthesizing yours; a suspicion of infinite, nested worlds...

I'd fallen further since.

I had plunged my hand into the prickly stiff pot-pouri of Libby's knicker drawer and pulled out a plum suspender belt — and said what a bad boy am I. I'd stood at the top of a multistorey carpark and heard the death music of my genes. Sexual longing for Libby was something I no longer troubled to hide from myself.

The phone rang and this time it was Boy. 'Where were you today?'

'Bit of a cold.' I forced a cough.

'I've sent her a parcel.'

'I'm looking at it.'

'So what's going on?'

I told him about Amy's sudden worsening. 'Libby's up at the hospital with her now. It might delay things a bit, but don't worry, we had a long conversation about you today and really cleared a few things up.'

'Glad to hear it.'

'Really cleared a few things up...'

When I put down the phone it rang again straight away.

'Okay, I've managed to talk to someone about you – no, not *you* directly – just happened to get chatting to this young doctor (I bet you did) and told him that a friend of mine had a son who... (they always fall for that one, right?)... And anyway, the good news is that it probably *is* a phase – but it might be an idea if you got professional help.'

'A shrink? No way.'

'Why not? Normally we'd have to go through Summerbee, the proper procedure and all that; but I explained the situation to this young chap and there might just be a way of...'

That was Libby: where there was a willy, there was a wangle.

I stared incredulously at the telephone receiver, at the six little holes from which the squeezed, Mickey Mouse voice continued to shrill. She just didn't get it. I put the instrument to my mouth again. 'Mother,' I said. 'Is that the first thing that occurs to you when a problem comes up: *how can I shag my way out of this one?* You're unbelievable. I fucking hate you.' Then I put the receiver down.

And those were the last words I ever spoke to her.

You would have said at a glance that the girl in the porch was about twenty-five.

'Is that you?'

'No wonder you can't see me, it's so dark. Why don't you put a few lights on?'

I threw a switch. She looked pale, but that might just have been foundation. Whatever – it made her seem less healthful, less wholesome, and along with the caked make-up, older. She had on the angora dress under Colin Garganey's jacket, which I noticed she seemed to have retained despite the breakup.

'Were you on the way to somewhere?'

'No.'

'Libby's not here.'

'I know.'

The sky behind her head was moonfree but star bright, Orion rising over the violently wagging tongues of treetops.

'Well, can I come in then?' Anne said peevishly. 'It's freezing out here.'

'I'd rather you didn't. Things are a bit difficult.'

'I heard. Libby phoned me from the hospital... Look, let me in.' Her teeth were chattering.

I stood aside, gesturing towards the cave warmth of the sitting room.

Once inside, she made straight for the fire, holding supplicatory palms towards the flames.

'You're bloody thin,' I observed.

She snorted derision.

'Well, you are.'

Temper blazed suddenly. 'Oh yeah!' Casting aside Colin's jacket, she stood defiantly erect. The angora dress hung from her shoulders in straight lines. Breasts, which had blown up so suddenly, were on the way out. Fleshless thighs bowed between the knees and the point where they met again at some unimaginable distance above the hem line. '*Look* at me. Jumbo the elephant!' I looked. She was the opposite of elephantine. I mean, she was thin. She had gone past model thin and was on her way to *Three Towers at Treblinka* thin. Only, she didn't know it.

Eventually she slid down to a sitting position, joints cracking, and I perched on the arm of a nearby chair. 'So what do you want?'

A pause.

'It was Libby's idea. We thought you might need a bit of company tonight.' She patted the rug beside her.

'So she told you?'

'Uh-uh.'

'How much did she tell you?' I looked at her closely. Groaned.

'At least you've got a mother who cares about you. She's worried sick.'

'Just fuck off, will you, Anne.'

'Look there's no need to be like that. I want to help.'

'Oh, do you? How can *you* help?'

Junk rings gleamed in the firelight as she reached to pat my leg. 'Talk about it. It helps to talk – if you don't object to spending your evening with a fat old cow like me . . . We used to be friends, remember? What happened to us?'

'Puberty.'

'That's not the way it seemed to me. I can recall having to lock you in the house to get you to play with me – to stop you running home all the time to your beloved mother.' Bony fingers moved to the sketchbook, opening the cover. 'Are these Boy's drawings?'

'Libby told me that he raped you.'

'Did he? I must have shut it out of my memory. If I was to brood over what happened it would only increase his power over me. Rape is about power, you know, not love.'

'You got that out of a book.'

'No, I didn't, I got it from Libby.'

'Well, she got it from *Cosmopolitan*.'

'She's a very wise woman, your mother.' Anne turned the pages. 'Wise and beautiful...So beautiful...Who can blame you. It's quite natural, you know, Hal, lots of boys your age sort of...fasten on the nearest available woman.'

'Just my hard luck I happen to be related to her.'

She smiled triumphantly. 'So you do, then?'

'What?'

'Desire her.' The eyes seemed enormous in the pinched face, with its protruding cheekbones. 'Ironic in a way, isn't it? It makes you and Boy rivals.'

She shuffled closer to me and I shivered, despite the fire licking angrily around the coals.

'Poor, poor, Harry. If you just think about it for a second – what can happen? She's your mother.'

'I know.'

'She's not for you, not in that way. There's plenty of other females in the world.'

'Did Libby put you up to this?'

Her breath was sere, anoxic. 'Don't look a gift horse in the proverbial, Hal.'

'What do you mean?'

'You can be a bit thick, sometimes, can't you?' She gave me a shove. 'Going to offer me a drink, then?'

'Tea or coffee?'

'A *drink* drink, stupid.'

Lodging her hair behind her ears, Anne turned her attention again to the sketchpad, lifting the gouache-dabbed cover again with the smile of a superior being on her hollowed-out face.

Martin kept his snob wine racked up in the scullery. Like nothing else on the plot, these bottles had the power to make him happy: his Saint Emilions, his Pomerols ... Even Libby would never dare crack one, buying her glugging wine in Unwins and keeping it strictly separate. With the business crashing down around his ears, Martin's wine was about all he had left in life. I hesitated for about a nanosecond before pulling the oldest and dustiest I could find, taking it back to the kitchen and gouging out the cork. In your eye, Dad.

When I returned the lights were off and the sofa had been pulled round to face the fire, which threw shifting, sharply angled shadows around the room. The darkness felt expectant. Anne, the Yahtzee Nazi, having sloughed her dress, was curled up on the sofa under a blanket, waiting for me, but when I pulled it aside all I really wanted to do was weep.

'Well, what are you waiting for?' she said.

'Can I have a drink first?'

V

Just one look, no more than an inverted blink, gave me the message that here was a day to shrink from. A thousand neural shivers met in one sickening throb as I swung my feet floorwards and shuffled snake-eyes to the landing.

Overnight, consciousness had been redefined as a spectrography of pain. The stairwell, usually one of the dark places of the earth, was this morning an acid movie of accidental colours. Even the hall – whose alleged lightlessness Libby always fulminated against – braised your retinas with its blowtorch infra-reds and ultraviolets. Cowering behind a cupped hand I crossed the parquet and peeked inside the sitting room. What I saw both shocked and amazed me.

The cadre of deadmen ranged along the fender looked vaguely familiar, but the burst, down-haemorrhaging cushion? The shattered glass, the bloodstains? (whose blood?). Most puzzling of all were three neat pink cones of salt on the rug, suggesting a scale model of the pyramids at Giza.

From the general hubbub of pain one small pain, that of a cut finger, was beginning to make itself heard. Holding the clamorous digit up to view, patched with a sticking plaster that I dimly recalled fishing out of the first aid box in the downstairs lavatory, memory stirred at an alien aroma. I sniffed my fingers. Suddenly a vision came to me of a naked human stick insect, pouring table salt over the rug and saying, 'This'll draw the stain out.'

An involuntary gasp unstuck the tongue from my palate as last night's events came back in a rush. I put the sitting room back together as best I could then hurried to school, an hour late.

'And she had nothing on under the dress?'

'Not a stitch.'

'Obviously gagging for it.'

'Obviously.'

It was mid-morning now and I was feeling slightly less nauseous. I hadn't vomited for a while, at any rate, although the biology lab's reek of formaldehyde was giving me problems.

'Why you, though?' said Malcolm, his scalpel quivering over the gassed, outspread body of a frog. 'I mean, she usually goes out with six-formers. Aren't you a bit of a mercy fuck?'

I'd had sex with Anne, not because I believed that doing so would wean me off wanting Libby, but because not to do so, in the circumstances, seemed like bad manners. It was easier and kinder to hide the revulsion I felt at the sight of her emaciated body. So I had done it with eyes closed, desperately imagining a more fleshed-out pair of calves (coltish, even) crossed around my back, impressed by my own altruism. A mercy fuck, indeed.

'Sour grapes, Malcolm.'

Malcolm tore angrily into the frog. He'd been pissed off enough about all the time I was spending hanging out with Boy; and now it seemed just too much that I had to go and lose my virginity before him. 'She's a walking fucking skeleton nowadays anyway.'

I grasped the edge of the bench, as a fresh wave of nausea broke over me.

'Can you show me where the clitoris is?' said a classmate who'd been earwigging on our conversation. He leafed through his textbook to a well-thumbed page and I assented, queasily. But just as fountain pen was applied to diagram the biology teacher shrilled my name, causing a blot which no doubt spread as the book was hurriedly closed to produce one of those death's-head spatchcock vulvas I was always coming across in school textbooks.

Apparently Roseberry wanted to see me.

In the dim passageway outside the head's study, seated next to a trophy cabinet rammed with cups and shields, one or two of them bearing Boy's name, I began for the first time to feel anxious as well as just sick. There'd been no call from Libby that morning, the significance of which fact I'd had scant opportunity to reflect upon before now. Eventually a buzzer sounded and the study door swung open to reveal a sliver of red carpet on which stood Cowley's beckoning form, his tortoiseshell-framed eyes evasive. The reassuring squeeze of my upper arm as I passed increased my sense of foreboding.

'Come in, Housemartin,' said the head's voice. 'Sit down.'

Roseberry had his back to the window, a halo of fire about his mad hair. His expression was unreadable, but I sensed none of the usual stage thunder; in fact the atmosphere of the room felt unpleasantly inert.

'It's about Amy, isn't it?'

Roseberry rubbed his forehead and looked at Cowley.

Strange, the perversely admonitory effect of bland, unblaming phrases, the inner bracing that takes place whenever language is detected trying to peel itself away from the salt, the sour or the too tart. When he paused in his prepared speech for breath, I craned round in my chair seeking a second opinion. Cowley was shielding his eyes, shoulders oscillating as if with stifled mirth, only it wasn't mirth.

I looked back at the head. 'How's my mother taking it?'

A deeper, darker silence.

'Is Libby all right?'

He motioned to Cowley. 'Perhaps you could go and see if . . .'

My form master left the room.

'Sometimes these things affect people in odd ways, Harry. Most likely she'll come home soon enough . . . But for now, just to warn you, your mother is being treated as a missing person.'

'A missing—?'

'She wrote two letters, which were found among her

108

things at the hospital; one for your solicitor, of whose contents he has apprised the police, and the other for you. Probably best if I leave you alone for a minute or two while you read it.'

He got up from his desk and came and perched, briefly, in a chair next to mine, handing me a sealed lavender envelope. I smelled pipe tobacco on his breath. 'I'm sorry, Harry. It's a rotten thing to happen.'

March was still making unkeepable promises as Cowley and I walked out into the mild, still air. The only sound other than the radio of the waiting taxi was a bluebottle's confused buzzing. I wondered whom they'd chosen to see me home, hoping that it wouldn't be Robin: he was no good in a crisis, Libby always said that he—

Amy gone, Libby missing. Suddenly all the breath went out of my body.

'Steady, Harry.' Cowley had felt the lurch in my step, grabbing me just in time. Though he couldn't know the depth that had opened up underneath my feet.

Just a few words to help you understand.

Not so bad that Summerbee didn't pick it up, apparently. Easy to miss. She had something called CML, a type of leukaemia. Nothing they could do after the second attack but move her to a quiet room where she couldn't frighten the other children. That's where I'm writing to you from, a quiet, horribly quiet, room. Amy, or what used to be Amy, is next to me. She never came round, really.

With her gone there's really nothing here to hold me except you, and clearly you'd be much better off if you never saw hide nor hair of me again. What happened up in the attic today proves it, though maybe it ought not to have been quite the shock it was. Just chickens coming home to roost.

We like to fool ourselves that children forget everything, the little moments when we overstep the mark, but they don't. Through a combination of ignorance, old wives' tales and just plain – I can't go on with this sentence, I'm too ashamed. The cold way you'll judge me when you look at it all through adult eyes! When you know everything. All I can think to do, for both our sakes – for everybody's sake, considering the terrible mess things have got into – is to remove myself from the situation.

There's no proper way to end this letter just as there was no proper way to begin it, but the pain I feel is so huge that I'm scared I'll be overwhelmed if I don't do something quickly. Believe me, this is in your best interests. Loving you always, Libby.

'Where's the funeral darling, where's the facking funeral?' The cabby elbowed several tutting quavers into his horn, followed by a fervent breve. 'Come on, sweetheart.' Finally the stalled motorcade ahead of us began to shift and the cab, with its shot suspension, rumbled into Cato Road. 'Would have to be a facking woman, wouldn't it?' he said, deadfish eyes seeking mine in the rear-view mirror.

The cabby didn't seem to notice that I'd been quietly sick into the floorwell, but Boy certainly did (it was Boy they'd chosen to see me home); eyeing me sidelong, he kept blowing and wafting at the vomitous tang rising up between us, yanking his door open disgustedly before the cab had quite stopped moving.

'Want me to wait?' asked the driver.

Boy shook his head.

A series of shoves propelled me through the gate and up the path. 'I went up the hospital last night and your mother got me chucked out. I thought you said she was coming round to the idea?'

'It doesn't matter anyway,' I muttered, wiping my mouth with a sick-spattered handkerchief.

'What do you mean, it doesn't matter?'

In my addled state, I thought that he was coming towards me to offer a commiseratory shoulder. The blow was an unexpected shock. After the first they came with dull regularity; sheets of white lightning sliding past my face, leaving me with a headful of crackling kapok and distant bells bring-bringing the bad news.

In the end I showed him the letter, just to make him stop.

Lips moved rapidly as he speed-read the three lavender sheets. 'What's this mean?'

'She's done a runner.'

'Yeah, but all this about . . . ?'

Lying just seemed too much of an effort. 'I used to suffer from night terrors, terrible dreams. I'd wake up screaming. She used to take me into her bed to calm me down and . . . Well, she used to take me into her bed.'

'And what?'

'You know, talk to me. Fuck it: she used to play with my penis. Once or twice she may even have . . . sucked it.'

'Sucked your—?'

'It stopped when I was six or seven. I was over the

111

nightmares by then...To tell the truth I'd started faking them. What?'

He was giving me that abattoir stare again. 'That's why you didn't say fuck all to her about me, wasn't it? Fucking pervert: you wanted to keep her all to yourself... You've been stringing me along, you little cunt.'

I was halfway down the path before he caught up, tackling low and slinging me into touch under the buddleia. Following, crashing through the bush, the whole hot bulk of him bore down. He smelled of fags and stick deodorant. A hand on the back of my head crushed my face into frost-baked soil and cartilage gave with an audible crack.

But just as my taste buds were registering the metallic tang of blood, he suddenly stiffened and clamped a hand over my mouth. In the ensuing silence I heard, we both heard, the click of the front gate.

Through a gap in the tangle of shrubbery a pair of grey leather shoes came by us along the path; a pair of polyester trouser bottoms alive with static, clinging to their owner's leg hairs. I struggled to force some sort of sound out from between Boy's fingers, but it was no good; just breathing was difficult enough. Bubbles of roseate snot seethed from my nostrils as I watched safe hands in string-backed driving gloves set something carefully down in the porch. The pile of smashed wood that Clem had taken away had been painstakingly glued back together, repainted and repapered. He'd even added some cotton-wool smoke coming out of the chimney. I watched him knock and wait, knock again, wait some more...and then go, leaving the doll's house behind him.

When the gate clicked shut behind Clem's back and the snort of the Rover's exhaust fired up, that's when I knew that I'd really had it.

During the beating that followed I kept reeling back to the previous day up in Amy's attic and the fleeting instant, before Libby recoiled from our embrace, when my erection had come thrillingly into contact with her thigh. It had been a dreamlike, elastic moment. One in which the unthinkable had seemed temporarily not only thinkable but do-able. A lapse for which now – and ever afterwards, probably – I was going to pay. Wasn't it only right? Weren't these kicks, slaps and punches that rained on the back of my head no more than I deserved? Perhaps I'd reached that state of schoolyard lore where you turn queer for the pain. Perhaps it was concussion. Whatever, a laxity had invaded all my limbs, warm and fuzzy like the feeling you get on the soles of your feet when you roller-skate over badly poured concrete. Though soon there came a point where I stopped feeling anything at all.

Boy started wrenching at the waistband of my trousers and it meant nothing. He hissed and grunted in my ear for what seemed like hours on end about Libby – how beautiful her legs, her arse, her neck were – it meant nothing. Even the blunt accompanying stab of his flesh meant nothing.

My last memory of that morning is bodilessly surreal.

It's as if I've swelled to gigantic size, because in front of the one eye that still functions there's this tiny window, whose half-pulled curtains reveal a Lilliputian interior. There's a bed in there, wallpaper on the walls. Even a figure at the basin brushing its teeth. Then a Brobdingnagian boot comes crashingy through the ceiling and stomps the room, the entire building, to matchwood. Now I have an unimpeded view along the path from the porch, where I seem to be lying, only the path is where the sky should be and the sky... The sky is down. I feel myself falling towards it. Can I grab one of the cypresses on my way past? I wonder that as the boot comes into the picture again, hanging sunlit at the end of its back swing, freshly oxblooded, cherry red.

Tart

I

Off some coastal reef of self, mouthed in my sleep, sounds bubbled up that had once turned a face in a sunlit kitchen (where before had been all vowel soup). Mah. Red slit parting, teeth flashing. Buh. Labial plosives. Making those sounds, watching them bring the sun out on that beautiful face, had marked for good and all the limit of her, the point where I began. Now a longer separation was beginning.

It started with the squeak of rubber sole on polished floor, rattle of apparatus (everything portable rattles, everything in hospital is portable); then the voice of the nurse saying keep still as she stitched my scalp, the man from the CID's pencil shuffling over his pad, the chatter from the set in the TV room, with its news of countries too distant to care about. But with the voice I was so used to hearing every day, the voice to whose precise pitch and timbre small bones in my ear had been tuned since before birth, strangely absent.

Then, unexpectedly, the TV found something interesting to chatter about. Something closer to home. Cautiously, I let the light seep under my lids and found myself squinting at a blurred, over-enlarged image of mother and child, cropped from an ancient snap. My mother. Up there on the screen between *Starsky and Hutch* and *Jim'll Fix It* (for one tear-stained, regressive moment I wondered whether Jim might not be able to fix it for me).

Rivers were being dragged, sniffer dogs set loose with lungfuls of Mitsouko and liminal Libby notes. Meanwhile an adenoidal voice intoned that she had last been seen driving a mustard-coloured Volvo estate registration blah blah blah heading towards the Dartford Tunnel and would anyone who had sighted her since contact the Essex police...

That night the conker tree rapped its knuckles against the window and a hunchbacked moon passed the gap between the curtains (never properly drawn) of the TV room, throwing milky rhomboids across its chequered lino. Luna: slooshing the tides around like mouthwash, giving girls their periods (Amy would never have one), a place where wasted talents are stored in vases, a river to be crossed in style. In the state I was in, I could make no connection with that bleached light. It spoke of colour and meaning leaching out of the world, it felt ersatz, denatured – like the light in McDonald's or the register office, places where you feel cut off from both soil and spirit.

Not that I was lonely in hospital, exactly. Unless it's loneliness-within-a-crowd you're talking about. Visitors?

I was beating them off with a stick. Father Malachi came, Dr Summerbee, Robin, Malcolm, Martin came twice (though on both occasions I was asleep and he hurried away again). Even Amy came, floating upstairs from the Chapel of Rest, her intense little face appearing at my bedside while I was on the point of nodding off. He humped and bumped me till I died, Harry.

But the one face, the one voice failed to arrive.

When the man from the CID made his third visit in as many days I naturally assumed that he must be bringing fresh news of the hunt for Libby, but no. He'd come to worry away at the details of my statement like some Thames Estuary Columbo. 'Just one more thing so's I can get this straight . . .' To help him this time, he'd brought along a younger-looking colleague who stared, chewed gum and sniggered inanely at my account of the rape; the area – embarrassingly – that they'd decided to fixate on. 'I just don't buy it,' this younger one whined, throwing an attitude copped along with his fuzzy-felt sideburns from *The Sweeney*, 'I mean, if anyone tried to interfere with *my* arse . . .'

Clem did a fair bit of moustache-tugging when I described the interview to him. 'It's only natural that they're having trouble believing you,' he said. 'After all, Boy's a butch-looking sort of bloke, head prefect at Wentworth. Plus, Johnson's pretty close mates with DI Turnstone – that's the younger of the two men who came to see you, Johnny Turnstone—'

'Hold on a minute – how do they think this happened?' I said incredulously, indicating the graffitied slab of plaster on my forearm, the clotted stitches in my scalp. 'Do they think I beat *myself* up?'

He shrugged. 'From what I can make out they think you interrupted a burglary.'

'A burglary!'

'There were signs of a break-in: a broken window—'

Obviously Boy had wanted his sketchpad back.

'Some items went missing—'

'What items?'

'Three or four bottles of vintage claret, quite valuable. They can't picture Boy as a wine buff, any more than they see him as a shirt lifter.'

I cursed the Libby-instilled neatness that had made me dispose of those deadmen. 'What does *he* say?'

'That he dropped you off at the house and took the taxi on.'

'And the driver?'

'The driver can't be traced.'

'Fucking hell.'

'To be honest, they think you're a brick short of a load, Harry; what with the things you were shouting at that poor old GP of yours yesterday, and also...' he leant closer, lowering his voice. 'Someone around here told them that Libby was trying to get you some psychiatric help before she did her flit. Is that true?'

I bit my lip.

Anne came towards the end of my four days in hospital, sporting a new bob and dye job that made her look, from a distance, so like a winnowed-out version of Libby that for one heart-stopping moment I thought—

'Harry, you're going to hate me,' she said as she clutched her kneecaps in the day room, 'but I can't do what you ask.' (I'd sent a note through Clem asking her to make a statement about her run-in with Boy.)

'But he raped you.'

'Well, perhaps I *did* lead him on a bit, grabbing his prick like that.'

'He raped me, too. He tried to rape Libby. He's a rapist.'

'Boy didn't mean any harm to Libby, he loved her. It was a misunderstanding. And he says that he never laid a finger on you either.'

'So now *you* don't believe me.'

'Well, you did get that bash on the head—'

'God, he's done a real number on you all, hasn't he?'

'He's just so different since Libby went away. He's been sweet . . .'

I scowled at her incredulously. 'Sweet! And what about you and me – the other night: that means nothing, I suppose?'

'Libby left such a hole in my life—'

'Was it Boy's idea, the new haircut? Because you realize what he's doing, don't you? Turning you into his surrogate Libby.'

'Makes a change from being yours . . . Look, maybe you don't remember that night as well as I do. I seem to recall that it ended with you crying your eyes out over your mother. There's just no room in that equation for me, Harry.'

'And it'll be different with Boy?'

'Boy isn't her son.'

Truth hurts. 'Anne, when she called you from hospital: what did she say? Was there any indication . . .'

'She sounded pretty desperate. She said that you'd got

abusive on the phone and she didn't think she could be of any help to you any more. It was all put as if I was your last hope, really.'

'Do you think she's ever coming back?'

She swallowed. 'Harry, if this isn't a suicide note I don't know what is.' Burrowing into a small clutch bag she was carrying, a chain-store version of one of Libby's, Anne pulled out the three sheets of lavender notepaper and handed them to me. 'I'm sorry, I didn't mean to pry; it was just lying there on the path . . . I was the one who found you, you see.'

Bite the bullet, Clem said, you're not going to get anywhere with this.

Still I had no intention of dropping the charges. Deep down, I suppose, an expectation lingered that Libby – real Libby, as opposed to the black-moon-on-a-stick, Bizarro-world version Anne had become – would swan onto the ward at any minute and put things to rights.

And then the Volvo turned up.

Just the single shot they showed of it on the television – ineptly parked, back bumper drunkenly askew – seemed to confirm what all my visitors plainly believed, even those who couldn't bring themselves to say it out loud.

The car had been found in a lay-by close to the coast road near Beachy Head. A popular jumping-off point, added the announcer, with a shuffle of papers.

II

'Harry, Harry, what can I say?'

I'd spotted him before we pulled up, hovering by the front gate in the rain, hair plastered to his forehead. A dense black awning over his brows separated into individual Stalin moustaches as he stepped forwards to help me out of the ambulance.

'Relative of yours?' asked the ambulance man.

'Friend of the family.'

'Friend of the family,' repeated Johnson, bracketing my shoulders with meaty hands, eyes flicking intently from one to another of my own. 'Glad you see it that way, Harry.' He bundled me through the gate then paused while the sound of the ambulance engine died away, darting anxious glances towards the rain-eroded concrete lions of the porch. 'Is there somewhere we can talk without—'

'Bumping into Martin?' I led him off the path towards the garden.

'Tragic what happened, Harry. Everyone's devastated.'

'I bet Boy's crying his eyes out.'

In the summerhouse we sat facing each other across the narrow space between two camp beds whose blankets smelled of must. I took my right arm out of its sling and rested the heavy cast against my thigh.

'Saw the car on the telly,' said Johnson. 'Don't worry, son, she'll turn up.' Patting my knee, he turned his gaze towards the house. 'Nice place you've got here. Never seen it from the back – the veranda and all.'

'Libby hated it. Hates it, I mean.'

'She'll turn up.'

'What was it you wanted to talk about, Mr Hugg?'

'Johnson.' He ran a hand over his face. 'How much did you know about your mother's background, Harry?'

'Not much.'

He raised a quizzical eyebrow.

'Okay then, nothing.' My forearm was beginning to throb. It was time I took some more painkillers.

'Doesn't that strike you as peculiar?'

'I suppose you just accept things the way they are when you're a kid; it only seems weird later on . . . Why – do you know something I don't?'

He chuckled wryly. 'Oh, we go way back, Libby and me.'

'You do?'

'Surprises you, does that?'

'It's not exactly common knowledge.'

'It's not, no.' He shifted on the bed, leaning his face so close to mine that I could count the wiry hairs on the bridge of his nose. 'As a matter of fact your mother and me grew up in the same part of Hackney, less than three streets apart.'

'But I always thought she was...?'

That wry chuckle again. 'Posh? Nah, mate.'

Twenty white horses upon a pink hill: a tongue flashing behind carefully painted lips, instilling nimbleness, precision some poor children never muster (and, frankly, most couldn't see the point of round our way): elocution. Learned, not received pronunciation.

'*I've* never been ashamed of it. Okay, I've got the nice house, the car, the villa in Fuengirola, but you wouldn't mistake me for anything other than what I am. It's not such a big deal nowadays, is it? This is the 1970s. Back then though...' I noticed the gravel voice adjust itself subtly during this speech from generic estuary to something more identifiably *Lah*ndun.

'Did Martin know?'

'He didn't find out till after they were married.' Johnson looked towards the house. 'He wasn't pleased...'

Libby's mother, Bridie Dunlin, ran a sort of boarding house. Spoke in the same boggish brogue Libby would slip into when imitating other members of the local Catholic community (I thought of her Dana, her Terry Wogan). There was no Mr Dunlin. The feckless sod who impregnated Bridie had made off at the first thickening of her waist, leaving her to cope single-handed with the child and the boarding house, not to mention the school fees. Because Bridie was ambitious for her daughter, Libby went to a private convent, elocution lessons, ballet, horse riding – God knows how it all got paid for.

And what did Bridie get by way of gratitude? After Lucy Clayton, Libby moved to Chelsea, made that name change from Linane to the less Paddy-sounding Libby and more or less recreated herself. Ran for a while with an arty crowd, then netted the big catch – Martin. The wedding was at the Oratory and the East End wasn't invited. Not even Bridie.

'Libby told your father a bit of a story about his in-laws. She said they'd snuffed it in a ballooning accident: can you believe that?' Johnson wagged his head in the direction of the house. 'He did. I can just see her saying it ... Poor old Bridie, though. Broke her heart.'

'Is she still alive?'

'No idea. Somehow Martin found out that he had this Irish ... char for a mother-in-law and forbade Libby ever to see her again.'

'Seems a bit harsh.'

'Well, he's always been a bit of a law unto himself, hasn't he?'

'What about you? Were you fed up about not being invited to the wedding?'

'Nah. Good luck to her, I said. Did me a bit of good in the long run; made me get off my arse and work to make something of myself.'

'You'd been close though, before she moved up west?'

'She was what you might call my childhood sweetheart.'

'And were you still carrying a torch for her when you came down here?'

'You never forget the first one, Harry.'

'Why didn't you let on about the past?'

'Things were running nicely for her, queening it over

all her influential friends; she made it pretty clear she didn't want all that stuff going over. I wasn't about to upset the applecart.'

'I suppose they must have been a fairly useful group of people for you to know.'

'Some of them, yeah.'

'And you kept it from Lilith as well.'

He looked suddenly grave. 'That's a cross I'll carry to my grave. If Lilith were to find out now, see, that I'd had that up me sleeve all those years, it'd more than likely set her off on one.'

'Like on the night of the fire.'

He looked uncomfortable. 'Right.'

'Why are you telling me all this?'

'I just don't want you running away with the same daft idea that Lilith got hold of.'

'That you and Libby were having an affair?'

'Right.'

'Libby more or less admitted to me—'

'Look, what I'm saying is that I watched that little girl pull herself out of the gutter by her bootstraps and I'm hardly likely to throw her back there again, am I? For old times' sake: that's the only reason I held off.' He nodded towards the house again. 'You know I could have had you out of there any time in the last three months?'

'Yes.'

'For old times' sake. That's all it was. What may or may not have happened on the night of the fire was strictly a one-off.'

'But did you have sex with her, in front of all those others?'

'Don't push it, Harry.'

'You don't really believe she's still alive, do you? Or you wouldn't be telling me this.'

He made a small, regretful motion of the head.

'So... in that case what's to stop you foreclosing now?'

Fingers which had been worrying away at the curly hairs on the back of his neck worked their way up to a putative bald patch.

'Harry – is there some way of us getting out to the street again without your father seeing?'

The Merc was parked around the corner in Somerville Drive. As we approached, a figure got out of the back. I hadn't expected a picture of remorse exactly, but neither had I expected him to look so extravagantly bored.

Ignoring the limp hand he proffered I looked pointedly at my own arm in the sling, then down at Boy's rain-spattered right boot whose welt had opened a seven-centimetre rent in my scalp just five days earlier. Then I turned and walked away from him, back round the curve of the hedge.

'Here's the situation,' said Johnson, hurrying after me, grabbing my good arm. 'He's already left Wentworth. Got a place at college in London. He's doing a shortened foundation year at the tech and then off to Goldsmiths'. If the sod comes within a hundred yards of you in the meantime I swear I'll break both his arms myself, that's a promise. Now, turn around, shake Boy's hand and tomorrow you can ring DI Turnstone and drop the charges.'

III

Later, when I was looking into the face of my father, that long face seamed with despair whose eyes avoided mine, I would remind myself that it had been for this man's sake I'd done it. It felt like a betrayal, but what choice did I have? The Huggs were taking over. Martin was a commercial disaster area, apparently, an accident waiting to happen. He lacked the business virtues, which Johnson enumerated for me: persistence, cunning, bloodlust.

Those weren't the only virtues he lacked.

I caught myself sniffing as I let myself into the house, expecting what? Not this smell of stale air and dust, certainly, this reek of unemptied bins. Having grown up with a mother who kept discreet trugs of site-specific cleaning products in every room, who went round before *and* after Mrs Armitage had been — who, even when she was talking to you would be scanning your nose for blackheads, your sweater for lint – I'd taken domestic order for granted. The state of the place came as a shock. Five days after she'd done her bunk there was cobweb on the walls above the delft rail and dust covered every surface including the hall table, the leaves of spider plants and the banisters of the heavy wooden staircase turning upwards into shadow. No, if Martin wasn't a great businessman, neither was he a tornado of domestic zeal.

I'll never forget the taste, the lack of taste, of the roast he cooked that evening. Beef like old satchel leather. An excuse for gravy (excuse? it didn't even have a sick note). In hospital Libby's disappearance, Amy's death, had been easy not to believe in. Here Loss had a taste, a smell. Loss soured the air, turned the water. Loss pushed itself down your oesophagus and squatted on your lungs.

Conversation was desultory, lodged in the here-and-now, the do-the-next-thing. 'I've put the immersion on for you to have a bath.'

'Thanks.' Apart from one lugubrious look, accompanied by an equally lugubrious slow nodding of the head, there was no acknowledgement of our shared tragedy. 'I did visit a couple of times but—'

'They told me you came.'

'Good to have you back, anyway.'

Let's just try to get on with things, pathetic as the attempt to get on with things might be.

I wasn't about to upset the applecart. 'Who's officiating at the . . . at the—'

'Father Malachi.'

'And afterwards?'

'People come back to the house. It's all arranged. Your mother left instructions . . .'

'With Clem?'

'With Clem Arnos, yes.'

'Maybe we should clear the place up a bit.'

'Mrs Armitage is coming in first thing.'

'Doesn't she come in . . . at other times?' I looked around me at the spattered Aga, the pans piled in the sink.

He shook his head, chewing meditatively on a piece of gristle before extracting it from between his teeth and laying it on the side of his plate. 'Not any more.'

Giving up on piercing the carbonized shell of a roast potato, I made do with a mouthful of disgraced sprouts. I ate left-handed, with a fork, the cast resting on the table.

'You'll have the opportunity to renew your acquaintance with Franz Lammergeier,' Martin said, with an attempt at a smile. 'He's over at the moment buying Art. There's a new line of ceramics to show him.'

Hopefully Herr Lammergeier had forgiven me for getting vomit on his new suit during my trip to Germany with Martin. Homesickness had been, in my case, a physical as well as emotional affliction. 'He's coming to the funeral?'

'He met Amy when she came over with your mother the year after you . . . Libby and he hit it off particularly well. The two of them got on like a house on fire . . .'

I scanned Martin's face carefully, side-lit from the scullery (we were dining by the light of a single candle to save electricity). Was he trying to let me know that he'd been aware all along what a *cat* his wife was? I doubted whether he was up to that sort of game playing. Maybe the hapless cuckold he seemed to want to present was the real thing.

Dah. The tongue comes off the palate, breath thrown in a grunt through parted teeth. *Dee.* Time adds a second smiling syllable. At some point early on, in my case, a rising pitch became habitual, accompanying an interrogative finger pointed at faces in catalogues, men in the street and (this one always got a laugh) male visitors to the house: Dah dee? Dah dee? Dah dee?

The German trip. What a bundle of laughs that had been.

I thought about it as I soaked myself in a hot bath, resting my plaster cast – grimed at the elbow and faintly smelly by now – on the side of the old roll-top tub. All I could remember, apart from parking aspects of my lunch on the Herr Direktor, was that incredible longing to be home again. It was the first time I'd ever noticed colour bleeding out of things, the world becoming thinner to the touch, the air losing its savour, sound dulling, dimming. I'd missed Libby so much it hurt. Puked every morning, cried every night into my cabbage soup. Martin wasn't much help. For some reason he'd laid down that we speak nothing but German, a prohibition that he was bafflingly pedantic about. When I heard him explaining to an old schoolfriend we bumped into by the baggage carousel at Heathrow that our trip had been cut short on account of homesickness, it was the first time the word had been mentioned. Homesickness. Watching them knowingly finger their ties, I'd wanted to kick myself. Perhaps the intensity of my distress should have sounded warning bells.

Getting dressed I came across a photograph in the pocket of my jeans that I'd plucked off the ottoman earlier, recognizing at once the image from the TV. The uncropped print, in blueing Ektachrome, showed a rare family group. I was startled to find myself being screwed out by a ten-year-old version of myself. Why had Martin chosen this image in particular, I wondered, to show the world? Perhaps because he was in such a buoyant mood that day, by the look of it, spraying a bottle of Mumm around the orchard, racing-driver style (Mumm was not usually the word with him, either). Or was it the same thing that had captured *my* eye, the beatific look on Libby's face as she gazed into her bundle, the look that I had initially thought was directed at me, and which it made me feel irrationally wounded and jealous to realize was actually for Amy?

Seal barks rose in my chest. Eyes stinging, I limped down the landing, only to run slap into that peppery perfume on the landing, that smell which my nostrils had been straining for since my return: the smell of home, the smell of mother. I followed it blindly into her room. Windows must have been kept permanently shut since she left, because her scent was overpowering in there. When I opened the wardrobe door it was as if she had walked forward to embrace me. Fabrics rustled with hidden life. Satin and perfume and lace, all ready to wrap themselves around a living form. Racks full of shoes, shaped to the contours of a single pair of feet, waited to be filled – including a foxy-looking pair of black suede high heels ruined after just one injudicious wearing in the Christmas slush. Footsteps on a pavement, drumming in the small bones of my ear, the squelch of ruined soles. I felt a snake uncoiling in my guts.

Panic fizzed in the atmosphere like unearthed light-ning as I felt my prick fattening, lengthening; would I accept the charge? Bolting, I slammed the door behind me.

Downstairs, the French windows of the morning room were open onto the orchard. Martin was out among the trees, in shirtsleeves despite the chill night air, surrounded by a collection of brightly coloured pots and vases which he was tapping speculatively with the rusted épée from the downstairs lavatory. The new line.

'Dad?' Music swelled around me. German death music.

He turned at the sound of my voice. 'It's a new process: you pack them in salt when you fire them – gives much brighter colours.'

Art ceramics was a sideline that Martin spent disproportionate amounts of time and energy on and which never made any money; perhaps it chimed more with his idea of himself than Housemartin & Son's core business of toilet bowls.

'What's that you've got there?'

I handed him the photograph. He turned the print around and read from his own handwriting on the back. '*Der König von dem Wald.*'

'The King of the Wood?'

'A private joke.'

'What were you celebrating, a birthday?'

'Nobody's birthday.'

'Why is it dated then? What's the significance of the date?'

One of Martin's vintage silences followed: complex nose, long finish. He turned the print around and stared at the fading colours. 'This was taken on the day of my father's funeral.'

It came over me almost before I knew what was happening. Another episode of blurt, another of those wildlife documentary moments – involuntary, reflexive. 'Why were you never *there*, Dad? If you'd just been around a bit more maybe none of this would have happened. Libby wouldn't have messed around with other men, she wouldn't have fucked me up so badly, she wouldn't have run away... All because you had to be such a fucking...'

I hadn't noticed any increase of force or pace in his tapping. It wasn't as if he'd hit the thing particularly hard. But one moment we were looking at a green vase with yellow stripes and the next his swordpoint was stirring the breeze in the place where it had been.

The breeze freshened, blowing away some of the greyish pile of dust that the vase had become so abruptly, snatching the photograph from his loosening grip. Martin watched it fly across the dark air under the trees, eyes drawn with a watchful, almost suspicious look to the fringes of his little wood.

IV

'Look, Dad, our trees!' I'd cried as we soared over the estuary – this was the way to see the world. From up here it all looked richly purposeful, cars pumping white and haemoglobin red out along the arterial. Our own little capillary was clearly marked by its row of cypresses, standing out like exclamation marks: !!!!!

'*Look*, Dad!'

'Nehmen mir Vati.'

'Dad, it's only a game, right?'

'Was sagst du? Ich verstehe nicht – sprech Deutsch.'

Unnoticed in the confusion of packing and driving to the airport, in the adrenaline rush of take-off, an abscess ulcer had begun erupting in my mouth. By the time we were through German customs I could barely speak, in either language. Still my father was bafflingly insistent: *Englisch verboten*. I didn't know the words for tongue or ulcer, I didn't know the words for I'm in tremendous pain and you're a complete arsehole. Without dictionary or phrase book all I could summon up was this single word: *Schmerz* – difficult enough to pronounce with a volcano under your tongue. Pointing throatwards I slobbered *Schmerz* until Martin finally got the message, locating a homoeopath who gave me some disgusting paste to rub on my gums, like charcoal chips in Savlon, together with directions for its use that I didn't fully understand but was by now too intimidated to have translated. The *Schmerz* disappeared all right, but the paste – at least in the quantities I was whacking it on – induced a swimmy-headed, nauseous state. And did I know the German for a swimmy-headed, nauseous state?

Next day, five minutes into our tour of the Lammergeier Gesellschaft works, it came to me that I didn't.

'Herr Lammergeier?'

I didn't recognize him at first. Not until, pausing in his flow, he covered his suit breast with both hands, winked and said to me in a low voice that might have been mistaken by passers-by for tones of condolence, 'Please don't vomit over this one, Harry, it's the only suit I've brought with me.'

I was standing, blinking, with Father Malachi in the Garden of Remembrance at Southchurch crematorium. Amy's funeral service had just finished. We'd been discussing *The Stolen Child*, the poem by W. B. Yeats that Libby had chosen to be read, when suddenly I became aware that we were three.

'It feels indeed like a theft, doesn't it? Such a bright

little thing, such a strong *will*. Had she survived we would have heard great things from that little person, there's no doubt of it...'

He looked younger than I remembered, roguish in his sleek suit and arty spectacle frames. 'Sorry for bringing that up,' he said, once Father Malachi had peeled away. '*Schade*, no pun intended – it must have been very distressing for you at the time... And you were missing your mother. As now. An extraordinary woman your mother. When she was over the year after with little Amy – God rest her soul – she charmed everyone... And such an eye. She sniffed out at once the good things in my collection. Now there is a woman who could tell, as the Americans say, shit from Shinola.'

'She knew a load of painters at one time,' I said, remembering a blush-making exhibition I'd been dragged round at the Whitechapel, by an artist she'd once modelled for.

'I think it was a gift. Maybe you have inherited that gift along with her looks – you certainly have her looks. I am sure everybody tells you, but there is a quite extraordinary resemblance... So what happens next? Nobody has given me this information—' A pointed look at Martin, who was standing a little away off from us, pretending to listen to Imelda Parks.

'Back to the house.'

'Ah, the house. I'm looking forward to seeing it. I have not the faintest idea where it is, however.'

'I'll show you.'

Anything to avoid another ride with the catatonic Martin in the hearse.

Before we left I took the priest aside and asked the

question I'd been trying desperately to work round to when Herr Lammergeier had interrupted us. 'Father, did Libby ever confess anything to you about me?' But at that moment I was distracted by the sight of Anne, more Libby-like than ever in black, walking towards the carpark with the Hugg party – a murder of crows in their long coats – and when I turned back the priest had vanished.

'I understand your grandfather won it in a card game,' said Herr Lammergeier as we bombed back along the coast road in his hired BMW. 'Libby told me the story. . . How we laughed at her stories: the one about the three gold chairs, right! Such an amusing woman – it was a crime, on Martin's part, to keep her tucked away down here. Don't get me wrong, this is a lovely town, but it's a bit of a *was sagen sie* . . . backwater?'

I glanced towards a gunmetal sea running for once at full tide. 'I don't see anything lovely about it.'

He gave me a smile full of expensive dentistry. 'Maybe we are embarrassed to admit the beauty of our home town, just as our parents often embarrass us. Not that your mother could ever have embarrassed you, I'm sure. I bet you loved her very much; a quite remarkable woman – and especially remarkable considering the circumstances of her childhood.'

'I'm surprised she told you about *that*.'

'She told me a lot of things; your father was often busy and we had much time together – but there is no shame, I think, she was not the brothel keeper or even one of the girls. She just happened to grow up in the house.'

'What are you talking about?'

'Your grandmother. She was a Madam, *nicht war*? My God, you didn't know. I can see from your face. I am so sorry, Harry. That was unforgivable. What bad manners – you see my tongue runs away from me—'

'Well, I have a bit of trouble in that department, too, so forgive me if I ask you a straight question. Did you have an affair with my mother?'

He laughed a little, then considered a second or two before replying. 'I'm glad it's not so obvious to you as it seems to some others, Harry, but my tastes do not run in that direction.'

'You mean you didn't fancy her?'

'I mean that I am homosexual . . . Now, this marvellous new line of your father's – are we going to see it today?'

Libby's letter to Clem detailed arrangements for Amy's wake down to the drinks to be served: a Pouilly-Fumé, a Côtes-du-Rhône, beers for the boys and sherry for the old farts. Back at the house, caterers had put up trestle tables in the hall according to her instructions and spread them with crisp tablecloths. Rows of glasses waited to be filled from already opened bottles. There was a rail for coats. Food stood by in the kitchen, and uniformed staff were poised to wait on the guests. The place didn't look welcoming, exactly – the hall still said barn, though perhaps in more muted tones – but it was a definite improvement on what I'd come home to the previous day. Appreciation for Libby's forethought could be seen in the smiles of the inner circle as they turned up, relieved that she was maintaining, even at this remove, her high standards.

'I half feel she's going to walk down the stairs at any moment,' said Robin, coming in with Clem.

'I wish she would,' said Clem. 'I bet you do too, Harry.'

'But who's footing the bill?' asked Robin.

'Libby left money,' Clem replied. 'She's been squirrel-ling bits away for years – as young Harry here is going to be very relieved to discover, when he suddenly finds he's got nowhere to live. Make that call to Turnstone, Harry... And, by the way, how did you manage to get back here before us?'

'Franz drives like a nutter.'

'Franz,' said Clem to Robin, with a significant look.

The Huggs, who except for Boy had never been in the house before, stood in a black huddle, gazing around them with the frankly assessing look of tourists. 'I love these old places,' said Johnson, handing me his coat. 'Maybe you can give us the tour later.'

We followed them into the sitting room and I nudged Clem at the sight of Lilith, clutching an Amontillado and staring fixedly towards the top of the bay. 'Pink elephants?'

Clem, who had almost been married the previous year, shook his head. 'I've seen that look on a woman's face before,' he murmured. 'Measuring up for nets.' Once he'd mentioned it, signs of the mental tape-measure were everywhere. Strolling the orchard with his dough-faced younger son, Johnson laid out a swimming pool with baronial gestures. You could almost hear the buzzing of chain saws. Later I glimpsed Boy dragging Anne upstairs to check out the bedrooms.

'That's just *too* much,' I remonstrated.

'Take it easy, Harry,' said Clem, clasping my arm. He'd been hovering at my shoulder like a minder since the party began.

'It's amazing, isn't it,' Robin chimed in, gesturing

around us at waiters buzzing to and fro with bottles in napkins, trays of canapés. 'She's still pulling the strings, still pushing our buttons.'

'Who's pushing our buttons?' said Johnson through a mouthful of bridge roll, arriving at our side with a plate piled high with food.

I explained.

'Poor kid – c'mere.' Resting his haul on one of the trestles Johnson threw a commiseratory arm around my shoulders and steered me briskly away from Clem. 'Had a chance to talk to the law yet?'

At that moment Franz Lammergeier came out of the study, where Martin and he had sequestered themselves immediately on arriving. 'Have a drink, Franz,' I said.

'Thank you.' He picked a glass of white wine off a passing tray. 'So, no pots, Harry.'

Martin emerged from the room and paused at the open front door to dispose of a handful of greyish dust before moving off to another group of guests. 'I didn't know whether Dad was planning to tell you.'

'I would have expected nothing less from your father. A man of scrupulous honesty. *Dein Vater ist ein guter Mann.* He could have let me go ahead and buy the company, but instead he chose to tell me the truth.' He shook his head regretfully. 'Many a lesser man would not have done that.'

'Buy the company?'

'Yes. I was considering acquiring Housemartin & Son.' He looked askance at Johnson, who was hovering not particularly discreetly.

'Johnson Hugg,' said the Hairy Man, spotting his opening, 'friend of the family.' I dodged his wink. 'Hear you're a bit of an art lover.'

'That is correct.' Franz grimaced at the violence of his handshake.

'In that case perhaps I should introduce you to my son.' With a curt flick of his other hand Johnson beckoned Boy, who was coming down the stairs just at that moment. 'Gonna be the hot new painter.'

'Really?'

Franz listened attentively to Johnson's sales pitch. 'And you are at Goldsmiths'?' he said transferring his attention to Boy.

'From September.'

'It has a very good reputation ... Tell me, Harry, have you seen your young friend's work?'

'He's seen some drawings,' said Boy, with a smirk.

'What do you think, Harry? Has he talent?'

The volume of conversation in the room dipped noticeably. I was conscious of eyes on my face.

'I ... I didn't really see enough to judge.'

'No?' said Franz. 'But surely, even from drawings ...'

Boy glowered. Johnson had the look of a golf fan hoping by the bulge of his pupils to force a short putt into the hole. And then Anne's gaze caught mine, under the black cowl of hair, and something began to fob up inside like dark, cankerous yeast. I felt stitches straining, wounds gaping afresh. Angry syllables leapt like salmon in my throat.

Then a hand cupped the point of my elbow and Clem, at my side, whispered, 'Steady.'

'He's very good,' I spoke through clenched teeth. 'Draws very well.'

A collective release of breath. Suddenly everybody started gabbling at once.

'You must come and see his work, Herr Lammy-geezer,' beamed Johnson.

'I'd be delighted.'

'We'll arrange a showing, won't we, Boy?'

'Sure.'

'I'm up in London tomorrow, but the day after?'

'Fine.'

'Oh, one more thing, Mr Hugg, I'd like to bring Harry with me, for a second opinion. I have an idea that he has inherited his mother's eye. You've no objections?'

'None at all.' Johnson gave me another wink.

'So that's settled.'

'Honest, Clem, it's like being fucked up the arse all over again. Asking me to show him round the place like I was some sort of fucking estate agent . . .'

We were in Martin's study where Clem had led me, shutting the door decisively behind us.

'Harry, there's nothing you can do.'

'I just feel so fucking . . . Libby must have foreseen this; how could she just fuck off and let it happen to me?'

'Your mother did everything she possibly could to protect you.'

'She *abandoned* me. Why didn't she just leave me outside Sainsbury's years ago? That would have been kinder than this.'

'Don't get bitter, Harry.' He plucked my half-empty glass off the table on his way out of the door. 'And don't drink any more until after the Huggs have gone.'

I slumped on the daybed, where Martin slept when he was at home, and stared morosely at his bookbacks. Father a dalek, mother a whore. A little later there was a small knock at the door and Anne slipped in, closing it behind her. 'Clem told me you were in here... I feel so bad about the way things have happened, Harry, I don't want you to hate me.'

'I don't hate you, I just wish you'd eat something. You're getting so thin I can hardly see you.' Her eyes were glazing over, so I changed the subject. 'What do you see in him, Anne? Is it the sex?'

'Hardly. He only does it one way, up the bum, and it hurts like... well, you know.'

'Yes, I do know.'

'I'm half on the point of believing you. He frightens me, to tell the truth. Some of the things he says... He's been painting me, only none of the pictures really look like me. They look like—'

She was interrupted by another knock at the door. This time it was Clem, telling me that Father Malachi was about to leave.

I rushed out to say goodbye, but the priest seemed less than overjoyed at my having made the effort. 'Er, you asked a question earlier, Harry, which I'm afraid professional ethics, so to speak, forbid me from answering. Secrets of the confessional, you know.' Blushing bright red he muttered something about hoping to see me at mass on Sunday and then bolted.

Anne left soon after, along with the Huggs. Herr Lammergeier didn't hang around, either. But the old faithfuls, the inner circle, lingered at the trough until well into the evening, hitting the sauce like it was budget day, rehearsing the old stories – 'That one about the three gold chairs!' said Cyril, collapsing into bleared, tearful laughter – and in the case of Clem and Robin, old arguments – 'It was the buggering Catholics who wanted the troops over there in the first place...'

Pretty soon, I noticed that we were down to the crew who had formed Libby's Christmas Eve party, slumped untidily around the sitting room, all dead drunk. Imelda had nodded off. Cyril had become maudlin and kept going on about how much he missed Libby. Clem and Robin would no doubt have been scrapping by now if the sight of each other's askew black ties didn't keep reminding them of why they were there.

'She grew up in a brothel,' I found myself saying, to no one in particular.

'She was a wunnerful woman,' said Cyril.

'But I din' know she grew up in a brothel.' I tottered to my feet.

'She was a wunnerful woman all the same – God, I miss her...'

'Where you going, Harry?' said Clem warily.

'I've gotter find my father. Things I gotter say.'

'Just don't say anything you might regret later – you know what trouble that tongue of yours gets you in.'

I found Martin alone in the scullery, washing ashtrays and staring blindly out of the small window above the sink into the pitch dark.

'Father, I gotter say some things. Franz – Herr Lammergeier tole me something and I gotter—' He wasn't listening.

'Do you remember Ernst, at all; your grandfather?'

A wily, wrinkled face with nostrils full of shaving brush.

'You can't have forgotten the conjuring tricks he used to do?'

I slumped into a seat at the kitchen table, remembering my grandfather's shitbreath. 'He used to find money behind my ears.'

'He used to find money in all sorts of places. He won this house in a game of poker.'

'I know.'

'The poor fellow who lost it hanged himself from that quince tree over there. The architect.'

'I know that.'

'I wouldn't have put it past Ernst to have palmed an ace or two. In fact I'm fairly convinced he did. Some things are poisoned at the root, Harry. The Buddhists have this thing called karma—'

'Instant Karma gonna get ya,' I belched.

'It's not that different from what the dreaded Catholics call Grace – Hail, Libby, full of grace – not that your mother was the best Catholic. She certainly wasn't in a state of grace when she came to me. When we married she was already pregnant with you – something I didn't know until my father told me, much later. How did he know? Because he was the one responsible.'

Drunk as I was, this revelation made me sit up. I was conscious of a deeply stupid look on my face as I stared at him.

'She was sleeping with him up until two days before the wedding – she was his mistress, Harry; and I never knew. Father set me up. Talked your mother into marrying me, because he was afraid that I was going to quit the business and do what I really wanted to do, which was become a sculptor. With a wife and child I would need money. I would have to settle for a job in the family firm. He knew me so well you see, my stupid sense of duty. It worked. I gave up art college and devoted myself to earning money for her to spend on shoes. The whole thing worked out perfectly and there was no real need for him ever to have told me. But he did. Why? Out of sheer bloody spite. The day of his funeral I opened a bottle of champagne and—'

'Bad karma,' I gulped out, 'dancing on his grave like that.' I felt I had to say something, just to prove to myself that I existed, that I was actually in the room with him, listening to him say these things.

He turned abruptly and focused on me with intimidating attention. 'Harry. Do you understand what I'm saying? Do you have any conception of how sorry I feel—?'

'Sorry? *You* didn't do anything,' I blurted, wishing he would look away. 'It was them, it was—'

'That's just the trouble: I *didn't* do anything. I played along. Never said a dicky-bird . . . I never said a bloody word, not one . . . bloody . . .' He turned and began to bash the edge of the sink furiously with his washing up brush. 'Not . . . one . . . bloody . . . fucking . . .' I looked on horrified. Finally the head flew off the brush and his words melted into sobs. Arms fell limp from his sagging shoulders.

Getting to my feet, I knocked the chair over behind me. 'Dad—'

'I'm not your father, Harry. I only had one blood child and . . .' His face, now wet with tears, was all pulled down on one side, I noticed.

Then a sudden handbrake turn.

'Who's that?' Abruptly he whirled towards the dark space by the back door, where I couldn't see. The wind often caught the larder door, getting in through the broken window catch. 'Is that you?' he said, a smile spreading over the animate half of his face. 'How was it, darling? Good night out? Kept the wolves at bay, I hope...'

Stroke. The word has an affectionate, soothing sound which the real thing lacks. Life had dealt my father a minor stroke, although I didn't realize it at the time. I thought he was just drunk and confused. He went to bed (with my help) and stayed there for a few days, and when he got up again he seemed just like his old self: taciturn, evasive. I felt reassured. Then a few weeks later he collapsed on the front path and had to be taken to hospital.

They put him in a nursing home once it was clear that he wasn't going to get any better. I visited him fairly regularly, though he seemed to have difficulty remembering my name, occasionally shied peanut shells at my head and flew into irrational, speechless rages. The candour of that evening was never repeated. After a brief, embarrassing moment of clarity, the King of the Wood shuffled back into the boscage for good.

I might have put it down to drink, that initial outburst, but it was nonetheless terrifying. The appalling things he told me seemed secondary in appallingness to the clear indication that he was no longer a fit person to look after me. This was closely followed by the realization that there existed, in fact, no competent person to whom that duty now fell. I was fifteen years old and an orphan.

After I'd put Martin to bed, I reached out, as all scared children reach out in the dark, for mother. I went up to

Libby's room and hung around there for an hour or two. Tried on a few of her old clothes. The way you do. Sitting at her dressing table, sporadically erect, trembling with fear, I made myself up: Franz was right, the resemblance was really quite something, especially by candlelight, peering into the shot silvering of her wardrobe mirror. It could have *been* her.

'What was all that about, darling?' she said when she slumped into a chair at my bedside later that night. 'Dragging up in Mummy's old clothes?'

'Where the fuck have you been, Libby?'

She rested a half-empty glass of Pouilly-Fumé on the table next to my bed, lip-printed at the rim. 'Got an ashtray, by the way? Fags and booze in the afterlife, you see. Not all that bad really... Sex too. Budge up, sweetheart, I'm coming in.' Pulling the dress over her head.

'No.'

'See, you got it all wrong, darling; the knickers go *over* the suspender belt...'

'NO!'

'Come on, sweetheart.'

I wake up in a muck sweat screaming, coming.

V

The sea was running at full tide again when Franz Lammergeier drove us to Boy's studio two days later. 'Ah, the sea, the sea,' he said breezily.

'It's still the Thames as far as the pier, officially. That's the limit of the Port of London Authority's jurisdiction.'

'Where the sweet meets the salt. And what's beyond the pier? On land, I mean.'

'The Golden Mile, Shoebury, Foulness.'

'Such evocative names . . . Tell me, what do you think we shall see this morning? Will it be worth our while?'

'Don't know. It'll be figurative. Female nudes . . . I think we're going to see a load of pictures of my mother, to tell the truth.'

'Will that be upsetting for you?'

'Don't know.'

We parked a couple of hundred yards short of the

pierhead and crossed the road to Boy's studio, an old fisherman's arch with a low curving ceiling. It looked to have been whitewashed fairly recently, but already the damp that you could smell as soon as you walked into the place was breaking through in patches. Midway down the tunnel-like interior, Johnson was waiting for us by a table on which stood an opened bottle of Blue Nun and some glasses. 'Liebfraumilch?' he said, smiling intently. Hired lights on stands had been positioned to illuminate the pictures which hung around the wall: twenty large nudes, in oils.

'This is splendid,' beamed Franz. 'Such a lot of hard work, one can see at once.'

What I hadn't noticed straight away, because it could only be seen as you moved closer to the drinks table, was a tableau that had been arranged for us at the back of the arch. A naked girl – a very thin naked girl – sat on an old mattress staring fixedly into the mid-distance while Boy at an easel pretended to sketch her. The scene was so bizarre that it took a moment or two to sink in that the model was Anne Singleton. She looked cold.

'Feel free to look at what you like,' smirked Johnson.

Herr Lammergeier shot me a significant glance, then slipped his glasses down his nose and began to peer at each picture in turn. I followed him round. Occasionally he would turn and fix me with a neutral stare, making sure to keep the back of his head towards Johnson and Boy. Once he winked.

Finally he led me over to where Boy had now come to stand next to Johnson. Anne, ignored, continued to gaze at the wall. 'Excellent,' said Franz, 'thank you so much. You have gone to such trouble.'

'Not at all,' said Johnson. 'But – what do you think?' You could almost hear the sweat breaking out on his shirtback.

'Do I want to buy, you mean?' He turned to me. 'Could I make a good investment here, Harry?'

I felt panicky, searching his expression for a hint. What was the right answer? His earlier friendliness seemed entirely to have disappeared. 'That's difficult to say: there's no price on anything, for a start.'

'Just give us your subjective opinion, your – how do you say? – gut instinct. What do you really feel about what is happening here, Harry?'

'Technically they're very good. You can't fault the handling, use of colour, perspective—'

'Everything's bullshit before the but,' said Johnson, with a hideous false laugh.

'Well, it's just—' I tried not to look at Boy, whose eyes were boring twin holes in my cheek. 'There's nothing particularly distinctive about them.'

'What do you mean?'

'Oh, come on, let's be honest, they're crap. Chocolate-box. There's no coherent style, no art-historical awareness – they're not even good likenesses, compared to the life drawings. Blokes without dicks. I mean, half of them don't even look like women. And as for having Anne sitting there . . .'

'Bottom line,' fired Franz, expressionlessly.

'I wouldn't give one of these abortions house room.'

'That's just as well 'cause you're not going to *have* a house much longer.' Johnson gave me a look of concentrated scorn and turned to Franz. 'Well, we've heard from the monkey, what does the organ-grinder think?'

Franz hadn't ceased to stare at me with a rapt, half-awed expression. Eyes still fixed on my face, he brought his palms together in silent applause. 'I agree with him. *So*. Lunch, Harry?'

'Blokes without dicks! Marvellous. A most impressive performance!' Franz clutched his sides as we walked back to the car.

'I didn't believe how little they looked like Libby.'

'Well, they are not of Libby... Come on, it's not such a mystery.' He looked at me archly. 'You've made a conquest there, I think.'

'What do you mean?'

'Blokes without dicks. I love that. Like Michelangelo he paints men and pretends they are women.'

'I don't get you.'

'All finished here!' He waved at Clem, who was waiting in the car for us. Clem had been invited to lunch as well. 'You mean to tell me that you've just been staring at twenty pictures of yourself and you didn't even realize it? I thought you had an eye, Harry! He's in love with you. Maybe he doesn't realize it himself but, believe me, I know about these things.'

'He beat me up.'

'Sometimes we punch people when we'd much rather kiss them. No, Boy is clearly of my kind. I knew it straight away. Perhaps I should seduce him—' He turned at the sound of an animal snarl from across the street. 'Only I'm not sure he is completely stable.'

Across the road Boy, the issuer of the snarl, was emerging from the door of his studio restrained from behind by Johnson, who had one arm looped around his neck and the other around his waist. 'He's not fucking worth it, Son,' Johnson remonstrated in a loud voice as he tried to drag Boy back inside. They made a slightly comic sight; the tall well-built youth and his squat father locked together like that, staggering slowly forwards despite Johnson's undoubted strength and heft, impelled by the sheer force of Boy's hatred. There was nothing comic, however, about the look I saw in Boy's eyes as his head turned slowly in our direction. I had seen that look before, in assembly, when Boy had scanned the rows of faces in front of him, his eyes flicking back at the end of each row, searching for one face in particular...

Our eyes locked and he lurched suddenly forward, breaking Johnson's grip and rushing across the road in my direction. Horns blared. A taxi-driver with deadfish eyes set in a face like smeared newsprint almost ran him over, but Boy was moving too fast. I stood there, frozen in the lights of the oncoming train.

'You fucking little cunt...'

Luckily Johnson and Herr Lammergeier got to him before he got to me. Between them they managed to restrain Boy long enough for Clem to pull me to a safe distance. Though no distance looked like it was going to be safe for long: Boy's struggles were strengthening, breath and spittle seething, eyes rolling, limbs flailing. Luckily a squad car came past on the upper prom at that moment and noticed us. It screeched to a halt beside the stalled taxi and a couple of uniformed policemen spilled out, accompanied by the CID officer from the hospital with the fuzzy-felt sideburns, DI Turnstone.

Clem tried to push me into the BMW, but I wouldn't let him. 'That's the cabbie who drove me and Boy home,'

I said, pointing at the cursing occupant of the taxi, desperately trying to restart his stalled engine. 'Someone ought to nab him.' Clem strode off to do just that while I hurried over to DI Turnstone. He'd got back in his car and had just finished radioing for reinforcements when I arrived. 'Now do you believe me?' I said, indicating Boy's wildly threshing form. There were four men trying to wrestle him to the ground now, professionals, but if anything his efforts had intensified. I saw a boot go in.

'Well, something's got his goat, obviously.'

'That's putting it mildly.'

He was avoiding eye contact. 'So what's been going on here, then?' he said wearily.

I started to tell him. Noticing me talking to the inspector, Johnson detached himself from the scrum and came rushing over.

'Johnny, mate,' he called. 'Thank God it's you. Look, don't listen to that one, he's a fucking troublemaker. Mouth almighty.'

From the other direction, Clem was advancing with the taxi-driver. 'Turnstone, this bloke's got something to say I think you ought to hear.'

Johnson turned on me, hissing through his teeth, 'You fucked-up little loser. Don't think you're going to get away with this.'

The Black Maria wasn't long in coming, which was just as well, because Boy showed no signs of tiring. Blood poured from a policeman's ear where Boy had attempted to bite it off. One of his assailants rolled on the floor, clutching his groin. Even after the fresh officers had piled in, a broken jaw was added to the toll and bloodied teeth strewn liberally about the prom before the kicking, screaming Boy could be wrestled into the back. Johnson went along with him, cautioning Turnstone not to believe a word I told him as I was nothing more than a twisted little queer. Turnstone was avoiding *his* eyes as well by now.

After the van had pulled away I walked over to the studio with Turnstone and showed him the paintings. Anne was in there, wearing a dressing gown now. 'It was you, Harry, all along, wasn't it?' she said. 'I thought it was Libby but it was you.'

Turnstone scratched one of his sideburns and flashed me a look of undisguised disdain.

It took six officers, apparently, to hold Boy down while he was cautioned at the station. An additional two had to help administer the sedative so that he could finally be forced into a waiting straitjacket and dumped in a cell. He was still raging a couple of days later, when Dr Summerbee and Clem signed the papers to section him under the Mental Health Act.

'Didn't I tell you,' quipped Herr Lammergeier, driving us to the restaurant, 'mad about you.'

We ate at Oscar's in the old town. Over pudding I asked Clem and Franz's advice about an envelope which had arrived on the doormat at Cato Road that morning, containing nothing but a set of house keys: Yale, Chubb and window lock. There was a grubby label attached to the ring on which had been scribbled an address – 13 Sinclair Avenue – and below, in fresher biro, a time, eight p.m.

'Maybe you have another admirer,' said Franz. 'But hey, leave me out of it this time.' Franz had left a cap behind on the promenade.

'I'll go with you,' said Clem.

The address proved to be that of a nondescript terraced house on the wrong side of the London road, in a far less prosperous neighbourhood than Bearlands. Behind the front door, the house divided into flats. I let myself into the downstairs flat, and immediately sensed something familiar about the atmosphere of the place. In the hallway, looking through, it seemed to be just sitting room, bedroom, kitchen, bathroom. A small yard could be glimpsed beyond the kitchen window.

'In here.' A voice from the sitting room made me jump. At one end of a huge black leather chesterfield, the only remotely decent-looking piece in the flat and so out of proportion with the rest that I wondered how they'd ever got it in there, sat Cyril Parks.

'Harry. Glad you could make it.'

I tried to hand him the keys but he pushed them back at me. 'It's yours.'

'What do you mean?'

'The flat. In your name.' He wiped his old tortoise eyes and motioned me to an armchair opposite. 'Excuse me,' he said pocketing the handkerchief, 'I've been sitting here reminiscing... We had a sort of arrangement you see. I wanted to set her up with a little place and, you know your mother...' A dry cackle of a laugh. 'Why rent when you can buy?'

Uncle Cyril. Uncle Parks-and-Amenities. I remembered how he had wept for her at the wake.

'How long did this go on?'

'Oh years.'

'Jesus.'

'As a matter of fact I got the place by way of a gift, from a council contractor.'

'A bribe.'

'A finder's fee,' he corrected. 'Couldn't have put it in my name anyway: Inland Revenue and everything. Also Imelda doesn't hold with that sort of thing...'

'Not sure that I do.'

'Don't look a gift horse in the mouth, Harry...Well, that's it really,' he said getting up. 'Sell it, rent it out, do whatever you like with it – it's yours. I'll send the deeds round tomorrow...But I'd be appreciative if you acted fairly discreetly. Mum's the word—'

'I thought it was Johnson. I thought he was the one.'

'He would have liked to have been. But he was too much of a bull in a bloody china shop.'

'Did the others know anything about your arrangement?'

He shook his head. 'They'd have given their eye-teeth, any one of them.'

'To make my mother their whore.'

'Oh, come now, that's very Victorian of you – this is the way she wanted it Harry. It was her idea. She wanted something of her own, independent of Martin. Something she could hand on.'

'I hope she was worth it.'

'Her price was beyond rubies – your mother was an exceptional woman. And she had a good heart. You don't know how rare a thing that is, Harry.'

'I hate her. I hate her for doing this to me.'

'It was all for your benefit.'

'That's what makes it worse. I'm not even allowed to hate her.'

'Accept her as she was, Harry. We're none of us as good or as impressive as we'd like to be; everyone gets compromised by their circumstances. The world's a dirty place.'

I threw the keys on the carpet at his feet. 'Too dirty for me.'

Cyril shook his head regretfully. 'Well I can't pick them up, I'm afraid,' he said hoarsely. 'Respect due to the wishes of the dead and all that.' He started putting on his coat, which had been draped over the arm of the sofa.

'Jesus, she had a terrible life, didn't she? Everybody used her. Clem was probably the only disinterested—'

'Arnos was the worst of the lot, if you must know.' Cyril's face hardened. 'Is that him in the car out there? Pestered the life out of her. Rang every day. He wouldn't have settled for something like this: he wanted it all. Love, Harry, that old chestnut. Wanted her to divorce Martin and marry him. He was even prepared to adopt you and . . . poor little Amy.' Cyril dropped his eyes to the keys on the carpet. 'Got engaged to a perfectly fine little girl last year, but that fell through because of his obsession with Libby.'

'He doesn't know about the "arrangement"?'

'No, though he suspected she was seeing someone. That's what all that probing was about on Christmas Eve, in case you hadn't guessed. He thought it was Robin. Or Boy. She kept everyone in the dark, Harry, not just you.'

'I thought it was Johnson.'

'Nobody who was at the Huggs' on the night of the fire would ever have thought that.'

'Why not?'

He let out a compressed nasal sigh, like air brakes. 'Johnson. The man's a complete cunt. Libby was a tease, yes, but most took it in good part. People like Hugg just don't know the rules.'

Rummaging in the pocket of his overcoat, he produced a small package. 'Look, I brought this along because I thought it might be of some use to you, but as you seem to have such scruples about accepting things from me...'

'What is it?'

'The truth, Harry – the ultimate boon. The meaning of life. It'll clear up any questions you still have about that night, but I warn you: it won't make the world look any less dirty a place... Well, do you want it, you young ingrate?'

I shrugged, feeling out of my depth, then nodded quickly.

He handed me the package. 'Perhaps you won't thank me for it, once you've seen it, but it could come in extremely handy. We're all aware of the unfair pressure you've been under recently, so just in case there's any more trouble from that quarter, it might help to let a certain person know that you have this in your possession. Again, discretion, Harry... I'll slip out the back if you don't mind.'

I unwrapped the package, following him through the tiny kitchen to the back door. Inside was a plastic reel of Super-8.

'And he's thinking of running in the local elections next year: HA!'

A few days later I borrowed a tiny Bell & Howell from school, set it up in the back room of the flat, with its faintly lingering smell of Mitsouko, and trained the rectangle of light on the wall above the bed. A no–budget production, strictly home movie. Familiar cast of characters, Cyril alone not appearing. Well, somebody had to hold the camera, didn't they?

Open on a frame-filling close-up: black cowl of hair, carefully-painted lips, eyes with a hard dark lustre. She's dancing to music, although there's no soundtrack but the flutter of the machinery. Pull out to reveal . . . I'd know those beige floral curtains anywhere. Bearlands. Kicks off her shoes. Now she grasps the hem of her skirt and starts to raise it. Jumpcuts, in-camera editing, give the piece a racy, *nouvelle vague* feel. A leisurely pan round the room to make sure all the spectators are identified, slumped or coiled in attitudes of parodic adoration. A huge collective joke is being shared. Sex. Woman. Johnson is on his feet now, eager to beat the others to the punch line. Alpha male. Beer spills from his can and from his lips. His trousers are undone, a shrivelled namesake protrudes. Then the belt is out of its loops and he's waving it above his head, shouting ferociously. She's crying. Johnson thrusts a palm at the camera lens and when the film starts again the angle is different. The mood in the room has changed too. This joke isn't funny any more. Shock shows on the faces of the inner circle, but Libby's can't be seen, just her backside. She's on all fours and Johnson has a slim wad of tightly rolled bank notes which he's clumsily trying to insert into her anus as with his other hand he grips the back of her neck and bangs that black bell of hair against the radiator.

On the second or third time through I catch Lilith flitting briefly into the frame and then straight out again. Probably Cyril didn't even notice her in the viewfinder.

To wake up and find your bed on fire.

Aftertaste

The day room stank of urine. It was noisy too; the old girls rammed together around the walls in wheelchairs or leatherette armchairs chattering nineteen to the dozen. Some sang, some wailed inconsolably over unknowable griefs. Others stared sightlessly towards the sole source of light in the room – a wall, glazed floor to ceiling with sliding doors that gave onto a minuscule patio offering a view of failing sweet-peas and creosoted fencing. They were almost all women: senile, incontinent old women.

Was this what I'd driven all this way to find (with a broken heater) in the depths of December?

'Bear with me, she's here somewhere,' said Mr Kulchar, the owner of the home, his cheek muscles tense with a public relations rictus. He poked his head around bizarrely angled corners, evidence of the sort of cowboy conversion found frequently in these once-grand properties on the south coast. Women scowled at the dark face as it approached theirs; some even shrank as if in fear. 'Here she is,' he said finally, dragging me round a corner.

I had a vision of white hair and blue hand-knitted cardigan, slippered feet on the metal footrests of her chair. I didn't see her face at first; she was deep in conversation with someone on her far side.

'Mrs Dunlin, you've got a visitor.'

The look was wide open and welcoming, but also had something shrewd about it. She was old, all right; there were deep, concentric wrinkles around the watchful eyes – but a lively intelligence moved behind them.

'Who's this then?'

I noted plucked eyebrows that would never grow back, drawn in each morning with an unwavering pencil. The two brown lines tilted inwards like the accents in the French word for larch, *mélèze*, as she recognized me. Libby's smile.

'You're Harry, aren't you?' The slight wariness had gone from her expression, to be replaced by a luminous happiness. 'What a turn-up!'

She started talking excitedly, but her words were lost in the cacophony in the room. 'Is there anywhere we can go?' I asked. Mr Kulchar had disappeared.

Bridie got me to wheel her chair to the room on the ground floor she shared with Mrs Betts, the woman to whom she had been talking when I arrived. 'Senile, poor dear, like most of them. Not wonderful company … D'you know, a lot of them got syphilis off their husbands and never had it treated? Too scared to go to the doctor. Now they're all mad and blind … Don't say it, I know what you're thinking.'

166

What goes around comes around.

'You seemed to recognize me really quickly,' I said, thinking that it must be the famous resemblance, despite my dyed hair.

'You haven't changed that much dear.' She swept a frail arm around her side of the room. For the first time I noticed that available surfaces close to her bed, the mantelpiece, the bedside cabinet, a boxed-in radiator – all of them were covered with framed photographs of Amy and me, the most recent taken that Christmas before my mother died. I remembered posing for this one in the sitting room – a grumpy adolescent with his sulky little sister, clutching to her thin chest the lavatory from a shattered doll's house.

'Libby sent you these?'

'She wrote once a month, regular as clockwork – kept it quiet from your father, I expect.'

'And me.'

'Do you think *I*'ve changed much?' Touching her hair.

The question confused me. 'Have we met?'

A trace of sadness at the corner of her eyes. 'Just the once, dear. Maison Lyons Corner House in Oxford Street – years ago.' I noticed she pronounced it *Mason* Lyons.

Memory stirred. I remembered that day. After the exhibition at the Whitechapel, Libby and I had shopped at Fortnum and Mason, then gone on to meet some old woman at Maison Lyons. Libby had spelt out the difference in the two words clearly for me on the way but had not, I noticed, corrected the woman when she got it wrong. You didn't do that with grown-ups, you just pretended not to notice. Neither did you stare when people had pencilled-in eyebrows. Before she left, the mystery woman (whom I had been led to believe was just someone that Libby once worked with) had handed me a pocket book to write my name in.

'That was you?'

Bridie nodded. She'd even kept the page from the pocket book. Kept it? She'd framed it. I stared across the years at that childish scrawl: my naem is harry i am sicks.

'Can I offer you a drink?' she said, opening a locker to reveal a Gordon's label. On the bedside table, amidst the photo frames, were a single tumbler and a plastic bottle of Schweppes tonic, half a lemon on a saucer, its cut face dried. 'No ice, I'm afraid. Room service is just shocking.'

'Not for me, thanks.'

'Well, I hope you don't mind if *I* do: it's quite a facer you turning up like this... How did you track me down?'

'The number was in Lib—... In Mum's address book. Had it for years, never quite got up the courage... I spoke to Mr Kulchar on the phone; didn't he warn you I was coming?'

'Didn't say a dicky-bird, the bugger. No more than's to be expected.'

'Do they treat you okay here?'

Her eyes went vague as she sipped at her drink. 'Oh, it's not so bad.'

'I'm just up the coast, at university.'

'Are you!' She looked suddenly jubilant, then brought the faders down a notch or two at the sight of my hesitant expression.

'University, though. What are you studying?'

'German literature.'

'Of course. I bet your father's pleased.'

'He would have been, yes. He died a couple of years ago.'

At that moment the door crashed open and a weeping Mrs Betts entered the room, wheeled by a sour-faced woman in a nylon housecoat. The smell of piss returned with them. 'I'm sorry, Bridie, but she's gone all unnecessary again,' said the nurse.

My grandmother turned to me, dark eyes twinkling. 'What say you and I take a turn along the prom?'

Just over the road from the home was a clifftop overlooking the sea. A path ran along by a fence there, and this was where Bridie instructed me to push her, towards a distant cluster of buildings that might be shops. I gazed out at the Channel.

It was still a thrill, this unencumbered horizon: the Canvey-less, Kent-free expanse. But today fog had closed down all distances, there was no clear line dividing sea and sky to fix on. Occasionally you heard the hooting of unseen ships, passing as if behind a screen.

'Not up to much, the weather?' The estuarial deposit of dropped aitches and swallowed endings was there in Bridie's speech, softened though by a trace of Irish accent. Irishness was also present in a certain end-first approach to a sentence. It was a pleasant, even musical voice. 'You should visit the West, Hal: County Kerry. Those Atlantic rollers coming in . . .'

I pushed her along the clifftop through the chill, clammy air; telling her as briefly as I could everything that had happened leading up to and following Amy's death, Libby's disappearance.

'I kept the flat in the end. The house went, of course,

when the business was wound up.'

'I never trusted that little bugger Johnson.'

'Oh, the Huggs didn't get the house. Clem helped me see to that. We sold it off to a charity. It's a home for the blind now.'

We'd reached the shops: a Spar, a forlorn-looking petrol station and the welcoming orange lights of a pub. 'Why don't we just nip in here out of the cold,' she said casually.

It had a reassuring dinge. Inside I looked around: no fruit machine, no pool table, no television. The landlord (fat, braces, potato nose) seemed to know Bridie well, nodding amiably as we entered and eyeing me with discreet interest. 'G and T, make it a large one,' said Bridie. Suddenly I found the handles of her chair sliding away from me as, grasping the wheels, she steered herself to an accustomed table. 'Whatever you like for yourself – and put your money away. This one's on me.' Spinning the chair nimbly with one hand, she thrust a tenner into my jacket pocket, beaming. 'God it's good to get out of that hole!'

Over several rounds, none of which she would let me pay for, Bridie and I got acquainted. She was surprisingly candid about the subject I'd been preparing to tiptoe around. 'I've been no better than I ought,' she sighed. But she soon had me sniggering at High Court Judges paying top dollar to be ridden around like pit ponies. 'It's the only language that sort understands,' she shrieked. 'The Mason Pearson wielded without mercy... They was top drawer, my clientele, a little goldmine.'

'Why did you give it up?'

'The East End wasn't the same after Ronnie and Reggie left...' Join in if you know the words.

I showed her some photographs of my holiday in the Black Forest.

'Who's the girl?'

'Anne.'

'Looks like your mother at the same age,' she observed, 'only plumper. She's your girl now, is she?'

'It didn't work out. I have problems relating to women apparently – I'm seeing a therapist.'

'What, a physiotherapist?'

'No, a *psycho*therapist – you know, head doctor?'

'Oh.' Bridie looked nonplussed. 'The Black Forest, that's where your mother went for her honeymoon.'

'Was Ernst one of your clients, Bridie?'

'One of the best,' she said, ruefully. 'One of the worst.'

'I was his child, wasn't I, not Martin's?'

'Shameful.'

'How did all that come about?'

'He was her sugar daddy, wasn't he? Not while she was living at home, mind. I wasn't having none of that. He was always on at me to let him have Libby, since she was not much more than a child. She used to dance on the table to entertain the men, show them her knickers – but I wasn't having her going into the family business, so to speak.' A deep sigh. 'But she talked to the girls a lot; they were always filling her head up with their nonsense. One of them had a little son she brought in from time to time and I caught her showing Libby how to... Well, I won't tell you what she was showing her. Kept the little bleeder quiet, she said. Terrible nonsense. In a way I'm not surprised Martin didn't want her to have any more to do with us – once he found out what she'd come from.'

'So Ernst tracked her down once she'd left home?'

'She was desperate for money, though I didn't realize it at the time. Too stubborn to admit she couldn't make a go of it on her own.'

'I thought she had a job, in a homoeopathic dispensary?'

'That didn't pay the sort of money *she* needed. Linny was always extravagant, see. Had to have the best. The *money* she used to spend on shoes . . . ! Anyway she started sleeping with him to pay the bills and then Ernst hatched this scheme to marry her off to his son. I'll never know why she went along with it. I suppose it seemed like a bit of a giggle, until she cottoned on to what Ernst's game was, trying to force Martin into the family business, and by that time it was too late. Shocking thing they did to that man, the two of them. She never forgave herself for the hurt she'd caused him, and it ruined their marriage. She just had to make the best of things after that. You were the consolation prize, she'd always say. Her pride and joy.'

I went away to the bar to get a last round in before time. When I came back Bridie's mood seemed to have darkened. She was gazing out of the window at a sea of stippled lead, at darkness leaking into the fog like black ink. 'I've been a terrible woman, Harry. I'm being made to suffer for it now, though.'

'AIN'T YOU GOT NO 'OMES TO GO TO?' cried the publican.

Bridie looked at me. Her eyes were wet. 'I've got an 'ome,' she said, trying to smile. 'You'd better get me back to it.'

'Do you mind if I come over again some time?'

'Mind?' She wrapped a scarf round her head. Rain had begun to lash at the window. 'I can't tell you what it's done for me, seeing you like this, after all these years.'

'What are your plans for Christmas, Bridie?'

Outside I tucked my grandmother up against the cold and started wheeling her down the hill towards the home. A freshening wind tore at my thin jacket, knifing through to the bone, roaring then keening in my ear. The chair slid perilously on the path.

'Careful, Harry! Don't pitch me in the Channel, for the love of Christ!'

Just a twisted fence of thin stakes stood between us and a sheer drop. I peered over at the sea, beating the chalk cliff far below.

'Did she come to see you before—?'

'Yes. But I'm none the wiser, Harry.'

'They never found a body.'

'As if she'd been assumed straight into Heaven.'

It all came out then; my madonna-whore thing, the circumstances behind my breakdown – all couched in the jargon I'd learnt to throw into this horrifying vacuum. I tried to explain how I felt pity for Libby, love for her, admiration even, but how, in that complex of emotions, lurking painfully like razorblades in swarf, was a destructive, atavistic lust. I don't know if she understood what I was talking about. In some ways I didn't care. At university I'd picked up the habit of serial monologue as replacement for conversation. Other modes of the confessional, too – pecking at a keyboard in the dark, voices humming in my throat... When I left her at the home she embraced me warmly enough, at any rate. I promised to write with arrangements for Christmas.

Instead of going back to the car, I found my steps

turning to the cliff for one last fascinated peek over the edge. I felt a hand in the small of my back, a honeyed musk of breath tickling my ear. Life and the possibility of happiness seemed to hang, for an arrhythmic beat of my out-of-whack heart, by a thread.